Choosing Family

Book Five in the Boone Series

by Jim Hartsell

House Mountain Publishing

Cover Design by:
www.nickcastledesign.com

ISBN 978-1-7346738-8-3

Other Books by Jim Hartsell

The Boone Series:
> Pushing Back
> Matching Scars
> Keeping Secrets
> Following Frankie

Other Fiction:
> Tango
> Rock, Paper, Scissors
> Journey

Nonfiction:
> Glimpses

Children's books:
> Father and Sister Radish and the Rose-
> Colored Glasses
> The Box of Toys
> The Boy and His Mountain
> The Noise in the Woods
> That Doesn't Belong Here!

Children's books also available in Spanish

https://housemountainviews.com

Chapter One

Frankie has her nose at the top of the window where I have it open just a crack. We've been back in town for about a month and I'm ready to leave again, so we're heading up to Virginia. I remembered that Raymond and Charlotte were from somewhere up in the Shenandoah Valley and they said I ought to see it sometime, so we start north, just taking our time.

Up past Greeneville we stop for gas and to get Frankie out on her leash to look for a place to pee. I pull the truck off to the side of the parking lot, and we start walking. We end up a the end of a dead-end street, looking at what is probably the kind of house I figure Raymond must live in. It's the biggest house I've ever seen, bigger than the Binfield place, three stories tall and all brick and big windows. It's going to be something when they get it finished. A bunch of guys are swarming all over the place, laying brick and carrying lumber through the big opening where I figure the front door is going to be. It's noisy as hell, and a big part of the noise is these two guys about ten feet away from me going at it. It sounds like they'll be swinging before too long.

One of them is doing almost all the yelling and the other guy just gets a word in every now and then. He's getting madder and madder, though, and I think if it turns into a fight he'll be the one to throw the first punch. The loud one stops for breath and looks around. He sees me and Frankie standing there and says, "Hey, kid, get over here!"

He doesn't wait for me to say anything or start toward him. He turns back to the guy and says, "I've had it up to here with your lazy ass costing me money every time I lay eyes on you!" He looks over at me. "Hey, kid, can you pick that up?" He points to a some kind of bag laying on a pallet with a bunch of other ones just like it. It's about six feet away from me, so I step over to it and pick it up.

The thing must weigh seventy-five or eighty pounds, and it's all I can do to straighten up, but I don't let them see that. I stand there for a second and then put it back down.

"See that?" the loud guy says to the other one. "Just some random kid off the street and he can do the same thing we're paying you for!"

He turns to me. "You want a job, kid? I'm sick to death of babysitting this lazy ass," and he points to the other guy. He's still looking at me, though, and then he says, "Ten bucks an hour, cash, under the table, paid every Friday. There's only two weeks left on this job, and then you can go back to doing whatever."

When I don't say anything right away, he says, "Okay, twelve." He turns back to the other guy. "See? I'm betting he's worth more than you are and I don't even know his name." He looks over his shoulder at me. "Twelve, right?"

I shrug and the guy says, "You start tomorrow, 7:30. Don't be late." He shakes his head at the other guy, reaches into his pocket, pulls out a roll of bills and undoes the rubber band. He peels off the top one and hands it to him. "There's a hundred for this week, and be glad you got anything at all. Now get the hell off my worksite!"

The other guy grabs the money, gives me a look like he's about to jump me but decides not to and heads off toward where all the cars are parked. I hear him say something about "asshole" but I'm not sure whether he's talking about me or the guy that just fired him. Could be either one.

The guy is still looking at me when I turn back to him.

"What's your name?"

"Boone."

"Got a last name?"

"Hammond."

"Okay, Hammond, here's the thing. I need this job to come in on time, which is two weeks from yesterday. So if you're looking for a permanent job you're out of luck."

I shake my head. "Actually, I was—"

He cuts me off. "What I need from you is two weeks of hard work. No jacking off, no stirring up trouble, no nothing but keep your head down and do what you're told. If you can do that we'll be fine. If you can't, I'll find somebody else. Like I found you. Got it?"

This guy doesn't let anybody talk, not even to answer a question he just asked. I get a feeling he's going to be a real pain in the ass.

"All right," he says, "I got to go up on the second floor and check on the fireplace.

4

Remember, 7:30." He's already moving toward the house when he stops for a second.

"Hammond, right?"

I nod and realize he can't see me, so I say, "Yeah. Boone Hammond."

"McIntyre," he says. "See you tomorrow."

When I get back to the site after hiking back to my truck, the place is deserted except for a couple of flatbed trucks and a metal trailer. I pull in behind the trailer and there's a spot I can park in later on tonight. Backing the truck out, I head out of the dead-end street and go looking for someplace to buy some food.

The nearest drive-thru burger place is a couple of miles away, but it's not too busy, so we get our food and are back at the worksite with plenty of daylight left.

About ten o'clock or so I hear a car pull in on the other side of the trailer. The door slams and a minute later somebody with a big flashlight comes around the corner and sees me and Frankie. He stops dead in his tracks and pulls something off his belt.

"Who the hell are you and what are you doing here? This is private property." He's shining that light right in my eyes, so I can't hardly see him and can't tell if what he pulled off his belt is a gun or something else.

I hop down off the tailgate and hold both hands up about as high as my shoulders. Frankie is standing in the truck bed and growling real low, so I whisper to her to be quiet and say to the guy, "I don't want no trouble, sir. I just got hired for this job and don't want to be late tomorrow."

"Yeah?" He keeps the light right in my face. Frankie isn't moving or making any noise, but she's wound up tight. I can feel it.

"Yes, sir, just got hired this afternoon."

"Who hired you?"

It takes me a second to think of his name. "McIntyre."

The light lowers until it's pointing at the ground in front of me.

"McIntyre? What's he look like?"

I don't pay much attention to that kind of thing, but I tell him what I can remember and he finally says, "Okay."

He steps up a little closer and Frankie growls real low.

He stops where he is. "That dog bite?"

"She's just making sure I'm okay. She'll do what I tell her."

He says, "That's not saying she don't bite."

"She's never bit anybody, sir, I just meant that she's kind of worried about me right now, is all."

"Well, you let her know I'm not here to hurt anybody. I'm just the night guard for Mr. Brubaker's house, and he doesn't want people around that he didn't either hire or invite."

"Yes, sir, I get that."

"How come you're out here this late anyway?"

So I tell him that I was just passing through and ended up being here when McIntyre and that other guy were fighting, and McIntyre saw me, hired me right then, and fired the guy he'd been fighting with.

"How come you're out here instead of at home in bed? If you're working on this place tomorrow you ought to be getting some rest."

I don't want to tell him I'm standing next to the only home I've got right now, but when I don't answer right away I guess he figures it out. He looks at Frankie and then at me.

"Don't get any ideas about ripping this place off tonight. I'm here until the work crew gets here at 7. Tomorrow night you find a place to stay, you hear? I can't have you sleeping on the worksite every night."

He's talking to me like I'm some kind of homeless bum, and I'm starting to get mad about that until I realize he's right. At least about the homeless part.

"There's places to stay about ten miles further up the highway that way," he points up the road the way we went to get the burgers. "The Sleepover is the cheapest one, but you'll have to sneak your dog in." He looks at Frankie. "She doesn't make much noise, does she? I guess you could probably get by with it if you got a room out on the end away from the highway."

He looks at me, and Frankie, and into the back of the truck. "Harry might front you a day's pay to get a place, just for as long as it takes to finish the job." He stares at the ground for a second and then says, "I mean McIntyre. His first name's Harry. He's a good guy. How'd you say you two met?"

I tell him again about the argument and how I was just standing close by, and that's probably why I got this job. I tell him wasn't even looking for work, it all just sort of happened.

The night guard laughs a little. "Yeah, I can see Harry doing that. I'll tell you something, kid, you won't find a better man around here than Harry McIntyre, but if you work for him he expects a full day's work for a full day's pay. If you won't give him that he's not inclined to cut you any slack."

He laughs again, real soft. "No, he's definitely not inclined in that particular direction."

First McIntyre calls me kid, and now this guy. It's starting to piss me off.

He's not in any hurry to check on the rest of the site. He starts to tell me some story about him and McIntyre when they were youngsters and then stops, like he remembers what he's supposed to be doing.

"I'm going to finish my rounds now," he says. "You'd best try to get some rest. You'll need it for tomorrow." He circles around the truck and heads toward the back of the house, weaving back and forth around the piles of brick and lumber. In a minute the light from his flashlight disappears around the corner.

Chapter Two

"Hey! Hammond! Get over here!"

I look around and it's McIntyre waving at me from the other side of the construction site. Only my third day and already I'm starting to understand why Daddy came home mad so many days. The thing is, I never even planned to get a job right now, much less one that's busting my ass like this one is.

But here I am, pushing a wheelbarrow piled full of bags of mortar mix from the pallet to the masons, and according to McIntyre my only job is to keep up with them. "If they run out of mud," he told me that first morning, "they can't do anything. That's three guys sitting around costing me a shitload of money, so don't let them run out."

Frankie is in her spot under the truck, in the shade, just watching me push that damn wheelbarrow back and forth. I look over at her and I swear she's laughing at me.

"You stay there, girl," I say. "I got to go see what this guy wants."

I figure I'm in some kind of trouble. Seems like anytime he calls anybody over to him it's to lay into them. When I get there, though, he's talking on his phone and holds up his hand for me to stop when I'm about ten feet from him. He finishes in about a minute and comes over to where I'm standing.

"Listen, kid, we've got a problem."

I don't say anything, but I'm thinking back over the last three days and I'll be damned if I can think of anything I did that would have made a problem for anybody.

McIntyre looks real uncomfortable, but he finally says, "It's that dog of yours."

"Frankie? She doesn't do anything but lay up under my truck out of the sun. She's not in anybody's way."

I sure as hell didn't see that coming. I had figured it was somebody telling him I was too slow or took too many breaks or something like that.

"No, she's not," McIntyre says, "but you've brought her every day for the last three days, and yesterday afternoon two guys came up to me at the end of the shift and said they had a couple of dogs they'd be bringing with them the next day. Now, I know one of these dogs. He's mean as hell and chances are real good that somebody'd be bit before lunchtime. So I told them no, they'd have to leave their dogs at home."

I already know where this is going.

"And of course, when I said that, they said that kid, meaning you, Hammond, they said that kid brings his mutt every day and you don't say a word to him."

I don't say anything. I'm just waiting for what I know he's about to tell me.

"Well, I told them they still couldn't bring their dogs onto the worksite and of course they said what about that kid?"

I guess McIntyre's pretty uncomfortable about all this, but I really don't care. I've been busting my ass for him and it doesn't look like that means a damn thing.

"So, anyway, you can't bring your dog onsite any more, starting tomorrow."

There's no place for me to leave Frankie, and even if there was I wouldn't leave her all day long. The only people I can think of that I'd leave her with are Tiny and maybe Mark. I'm really pissed at whoever those guys are that want to bring their stupid dogs to work just because I've got Frankie here, and I'm pretty mad at McIntyre, too, right now, because he's taking their side.

"That won't work, Mr. McIntyre. I have to bring Frankie with me. She goes where I go."

He looks down at the ground, shakes his head a couple of times, and looks back up at me.

"Maybe you didn't understand what I just said, kid."

He's looking at me like he was at that guy he fired the day he hired me. I figure he's about to do the same thing to me and I might as well beat him to it.

"I'm not a damn kid, and you can take this stupid job and shove it right up your ass!"

He just stands there for what seems like a long time.

Then he reaches in his pocket and pulls out that big roll.

"After that smart ass remark I ought to just chase you back to your truck with a 2x4," he says,

"but I believe I owe you for two and a half days."
He pulls off some bills and hands them to me.
"Keep the change."

I start to say something and manage to stop myself. Sticking the bills in my pocket, I turn around and head toward the truck.

"Hey, Hammond!"

I don't turn my head, but I do stop.

"That guy with the mean dog was pretty pissed when I told him he couldn't bring his dog with him to work, and he was just as mad at you as he was at me. You know that guy I fired when I hired you? That was his cousin, so he's got it in for you already. I know he likes to fight that dog of his, so if I were you I'd head on back to wherever you came from. I've seen your dog, and I've seen his. It'd be a short fight."

I start walking again, not quite running, but moving fast. The thought of Frankie going up against a dog like that scares the hell out of me, and I can't wait to get off this work site and out of town.

We get to the main road and I turn north, toward Virginia, like I had planned to do before getting sidetracked. For the first ten miles or so there's a pickup behind me that looks familiar, and I'm thinking it's that guy coming after me and Frankie to pick a fight with us.

It pulls into a gas station and heads back the way it came. I look over at Frankie and say, "That was close, girl. Don't know how you'd do in a dogfight and don't much want to find out."

I settle in to drive and start thinking about the last couple of days.

Pushing that wheelbarrow around was damn hard work. I managed to keep up with the masons, but just barely, and Daddy did that kind of work his whole life, as far as I know. By the end of the day it was all I could do to drive back to the motel. There were two fast food places on the way, and I'd grab something for me and Frankie, eat, take a shower, and fall into bed.

"There's no way I'm doing that kind of work when I get around to getting a job," I tell Frankie. "I'd be dead before I turned thirty."

Daddy never stayed in one job very long, and I'm guessing it's probably because he did to his bosses what I just did to McIntyre. If I'd thought about it for any time at all I might have been able to keep my mouth shut, but I didn't think. I just went off on him.

Just like Daddy.

Chapter Three

Melvin's map says that I-81 runs all the way through Virginia, and the last trip helped me get used to interstate driving, so we get on 81 and head out of Tennessee into Virginia.

"That idiot McIntyre," I say to Frankie. "He lost a good worker by being such a damn hardass."

Frankie looks over at me and then puts her nose back up against the window, right at the top.

"Yeah, I know, I shouldn't have told him to shove it," I say, "but he could have figured out some way to let you keep coming without letting that other guy bring his dog," and as soon as I say it out loud I realize how stupid it sounds. He really didn't have a choice, I guess, and the other guy had a point. If Frankie was allowed, then he ought to be able to bring his badass dog, and I know

McIntyre couldn't have a mean dog on site all day every day.

Now, I'm wondering about all those times Daddy lost his job and came home all pissed off at the foreman or the contractor or the owner of the farm or whoever it was he got into it with. According to him, it was always the other guy's fault, and Daddy was the one getting screwed. Since it just happened to me, I can see pretty easy how all along it could have been Daddy being the one screwing up, losing his job, and coming home ready to pick a fight with whichever one of us crossed him first.

About 50 miles into Virginia there's a rest stop and I pull in to give Frankie a chance to pee and let me figure out what I'm going to do next. I'm not sure where in Virginia the Shenandoah Valley is or where Raymond and Charlotte live. I dig around and find the card Raymond gave me with his phone number. I figure I ought to call and see if they're even at home right now. I get my phone out of the glove compartment and when I turn it on it says I have two voicemails. The first one is from Mark.

"Boone, I thought I should let you know I got a call from your Aunt Claire. She wanted to know where you were and when I told her you were on a trip she more or less demanded your number. You'll be getting a call from her, I'm sure. Take care."

So now I'm pretty sure who the second one is from.

"Boone, this is your Aunt Claire. I'm not sure where you got the money to go traveling around the country, I just hope you're not into anything like your daddy was, but you have a sister up here you ought to be taking some responsibility for. Lord knows when I'm going to hear from Natalie again, and Hannah, well, she's turned into a little hellion. She needs her big brother to talk some sense into her before she finds herself in a foster home somewhere and—"

She gets cut off right in the middle of a sentence. I figure all I missed was more of Aunt Claire's bitching, but that thing about Hannah and a foster home really pisses me off. There's no way I can go get her. I don't even have a place to live, and having my little sister tag along everywhere me and Frankie go is no good, either.

I'm feeling sorry for Hannah right now, and I'm mad at Claire for being such a bitch, and mad at Momma for just taking off with that asshole Jake that talked her into trying to steal my truck that one time. Mostly mad at Momma. She didn't do a damn thing to take care of me and Hannah when it was really bad with Daddy, and now she's off who knows where doing whatever. Claire's going to just dump Hannah off at some office somewhere and she'll end up with somebody like Daddy. Or worse.

"This is bad, girl," I tell Frankie, "but I don't see that there's anything I can do about it."

That makes me feel even worse.

Now I don't want to see the Shenandoah Valley, or anything else, as far as that goes. I don't even want to call Raymond and Charlotte. I just want to go home, except I got no home to go to.

"If I had a place," I tell Frankie, "I'd go get Hannah right now and get her away from that bitch Claire. If she's giving Claire a hard time, then she deserved it. I wouldn't put up with that for a day, much less . . ."

I try to remember how long she's been up there. It's been a couple of years anyway, so I bet she's about ten by now. Maybe eleven. It bothers me a little that I can't remember exactly.

"That poor kid," I reach over and scratch Frankie behind her ear. "Everybody ran off and left her, didn't they? Just like they did me." I wonder if Claire is really going to kick her out.

I'm tired of sitting in this rest stop, so I get Frankie out to let her pee and walk around a little bit. There's half a dozen cars here, and one guy has his hood up and is standing in front of his car staring at the engine. He looks up when we get close.

"Know anything about cars?"

I shake my head. "No, man, not a thing. You got somebody you can call?"

He nods. "I was kind of hoping I could figure something out myself, but all I'm doing is just looking at the motor. Hell, I don't even know what I'm looking at, really."

He pulls out his phone. "Guess I'll call Dad. He's in the other car and usually runs about half an hour behind us, so maybe I can catch him before he has to double back."

"Good luck with it," I say, and he nods, but he's staring at his car and holding the phone to his ear. He's already forgotten about me.

"Come on, Frankie," I say. "Let's get going."

If something like that happened to me I guess I'd call Tiny. He's the only person I know who could figure out what was going on, but I'd hate to call him all the way up into Virginia if something did go wrong with the truck.

"Maybe we'd better head back south, girl," I tell Frankie. "We'll take a look at Melvin's map and see if there's anything worth stopping for between here and there."

I get the map unfolded and find where I am. When I trace back down towards Knoxville. I don't see any place I want to stop on the way.

Trouble is, I can't think of any place I want to go when I get back home, either.

"I think we need a place of our own, girl," I say to Frankie. "What do you think about that?"

As usual, she doesn't answer me, but I can't help but think she'd like it if she didn't have to be on a leash all the time. I hate the thought of using up more of Gamaliel's money, but I might have to if I can't find some kind of job right off. Thanks to that old man I can afford to look around a little bit and not take the first thing I find. I don't mind a little hard work, but that thing with McIntyre damn near put me down, and I'd rather have something that wouldn't be so hard on me.

Besides that three days with McIntyre, mostly I've done farm work, hauling hay and cutting tobacco, and I worked at the home with Mark and

Betty. That wasn't really work, though, or at least it didn't seem like it, so I don't know if I can count that or not.

The good thing about that work I did for McIntyre was that it was only going to be for a couple of weeks. I guess I could even handle something as hard as that job if I knew it was going to end pretty soon. I wonder how hard it would be to get that kind of job, where you work for a few weeks and then you're done. Take some time off and then look for another one. Maybe Tiny would know something about that.

I know I need to get something so I can take care of Frankie and not keep her cooped up in the truck or on a leash all the time. Plus if I had a place I might be able to get Hannah out from under Aunt Claire.

I'm not real sure about that last part, though. If I had Hannah living with me it'd tie me down to one place, and I really wouldn't get any traveling done even after all the work Melvin did with the map to tell me where I ought to go. Do it while you're young, he had said, before you got obligations.

I guess Frankie's an obligation, even though she doesn't feel like one. I don't know what I'd do without her. Having my little sister around would be an obligation for sure, but I just can't stand the idea of her in some kind of foster home.

If I go by what Melvin said, I need to decide whether or not I want to do any more traveling before I do anything about a job or a place to live. Raymond and Charlotte are on the road most of the time, sounds like, and I wouldn't even know where to start looking for Billie. I don't really care anything about Jericho and that crew. I wouldn't mind seeing P. J. and Joaquin again. Nancy is out there somewhere, but I wouldn't know how to even start looking for her.

There's places on the map I didn't get to, so I could go somewhere new if I wanted to, which I'm not sure about right now. I had plenty of new stuff this last trip and that was just a month or two ago.

And then there's Abigail. I only saw her for a few minutes one day and another few the next, but she sure got into my head. She's pretty close to home, too.

Then I think, you don't have a home, Boone, that's what got you started thinking about all this stuff in the first place. You don't have to go back to the same place. You could move next door to

Abigail, out to Memphis, anywhere you wanted to go.

When I start thinking about that the first thing that comes into my head is, I need to talk to Mark about this stuff. He's a good guy, and he knows me enough to give me good advice. Plus Gamaliel's gone, and so is Melvin. Mark's the only one left for me to talk to. He knows me about as well as anybody does except Tiny, and I don't feel right talking to Tiny about this. I'm not sure why that is, but right now I feel like it's got to be Mark.

"You want to go see Mark, Frankie?"

She thumps her tail a couple of times, so I figure that's a yes.

"Okay, let's get turned around and head back. We can see Raymond and Charlotte some other time."

We have to go a little ways to find an exit that will let us get on 81 South. Once we're on the way back I feel a lot better.

We're back into Tennessee by late afternoon and I'm getting hungry. We get off the interstate and drive through another burger and fries place, and I get an extra burger for Frankie. I circle the restaurant one more time and pull into an open slot in the back of the parking lot. It's out of everybody's way, but we still get a lot of looks from the people going through the line while I'm sitting on the tailgate and Frankie's having her burger on the ground.

"Hey! Are there onions on that hamburger?"

A car has pulled in beside my truck and a guy is leaning out of the window.

"Onions are bad for dogs. Didn't you know that? You'll make her sick, or worse!"

This guy reminds me of Abigail.

"I don't think there were, but it's too late to check," I say, pointing to the spot where the burger used to be. "She'll be fine."

He shakes his head. "You ought to take better care of your dog, man," and he turns to the girl behind the wheel. "Let's go, Bonnie."

She backs out, pulls away, and leaves us there, me looking at my burger for any onions and not finding any. I got Frankie the same kind, so I think we're okay.

It pisses me off, people sticking their noses in my business all the time like this. "If we had our own place," I tell Frankie, "we might could eat a meal without being hassled."

It's close to dark by now and I guess I need to start thinking about where I'm going to park the truck for the night, and that pisses me off, too. Seems like everything that happens to me right now makes me think about not having a place to go.

I hated paying for those two nights at the Sleepover when I was working for McIntyre, but right now a bed and a shower sounds really good.

Chapter Four

A few nights in a motel, a tank of gas, and feeding me and Frankie used up a lot of what I got paid for those two and a half days of busting my ass. It's got to be cheaper to have a place of my own instead of paying by the night. There's no way I'd live in town, but I'm wondering how much it would cost to rent a house somewhere out in the country. But I don't know about getting a place before I've got a job of some kind. And I can't take Frankie with me while I look for a job or I'll run into the same problem I did with McIntyre.

Getting Frankie is probably the best thing I ever di d in my life, and she's probably saved my ass more than once, but there's stuff I can't do because she's with me all the time. I hate even thinking about this kind of stuff, but it doesn't seem like I've got much of a choice.

"What about it, girl?" I look over at Frankie. We're still in the parking lot of the restaurant, and she's in her spot in the front seat. "Want to go looking for a place to live?"

She looks at me and then at the window. I think all she wants is to get moving.

"Okay. Let's get on the road, find a place to sleep tonight, and we'll figure this out tomorrow." Seems like there's always plenty of old abandoned gas stations around, so finding a place to park is usually pretty easy.

In the morning we get out the map and find where we are and where Knoxville is. Not that I'm going all the way back or anything, but just to have a direction to start.

Looks like Highway 11W will get us going in the right direction. It's on the other side of 81 from Greeneville, and I've already been there, so 11W it is.

When we stop for lunch I notice Frankie's keeping an eye on a couple across the way. We're sitting in some kind of park with picnic tables and a good sized playground. The couple aren't paying any attention to us. They're watching some kids on the swings and slides and I figure one or two of them must be theirs. The girl looks over at me and pokes her husband, I guess it's her husband, in the ribs. He looks over at me and turns back to her. They talk for a minute and he gets up and comes over to me. Frankie isn't growling or anything like that, so I'm not too worried.

He stops about six feet away. "Nice dog."

"Thanks."

"Does he bite?"

I don't ever think of Frankie as a scary dog, so it surprises me whenever I get asked that question. She is pretty good sized, though, so I guess it makes sense.

"Frankie's a she, and she's fine unless she thinks I'm in some kind of trouble."

He nods. I'm not sure he believes me, but he says, "That's a good dog to have around."

"I think so."

He stays where he is. "Anyway, we were wondering if you could help us out."

"I don't know, man, what kind of help you need?"

"Well," he says, "we're on our way to Bristol to see her mother. She's real sick, and we need to get up there as quick as we can."

I don't say anything, and he keeps talking. He talks fast.

"So, we don't have enough gas to get there, might not even make it to the next station, so if you could help us out we'd sure appreciate it."

He keeps looking back at the girl and over at the kids on the playground, so I say, "One of them yours?"

"What?" he says, and then, real quick, "oh, yeah, that one's ours." He points to a kid, looks like about four or five I guess, but I don't know that kind of thing. "She needs to see her granny, you know?"

"So, what is it you need?"

"Well, if you had a couple of bucks for gas it would sure help us out a lot." He keeps looking around.

I shrug and pull out my money. "Five bucks do?"

"Yeah, man, we really appreciate it."

I nod. "No problem. Y'all take care now."

He's already on his way back to the girl and she's getting up. Guess she saw me give him the money.

They're walking fast, almost running, and get into a black two door. They slam the doors and I hear the engine start. Five seconds later they're heading out of the parking lot.

"Damn, Frankie, they just left their kid there on the swing set," I say, and look over just in time to see an old guy reach down and the little kid jumps into his arms. He swings her up into the air and they head toward the other side of the playground. There's a picnic table with about a dozen people around it and they're all waving at the little girl.

"Well, I will be dipped in shit," I say. "Frankie, we just got conned."

Now I'm really pissed off. Here I was trying to help somebody out because I had a little extra money, and ended up buying those two liars a six pack or a bottle of wine or whatever. I start to get Frankie into the truck so we can go after them and stop when I realize I don't even know which way they turned when they left the park.

Frankie's real good about knowing if people are mean or dangerous. After New Orleans and now this, I'm thinking maybe she's not so good with liars. Guess it would be too much to hope for that she could tell if somebody was telling the truth.

"All right, girl, looks like we just lost five bucks," I say to her. "Let's get back on the road."

While we're on 11W heading toward some place called Morristown, I'm thinking about the couple that just stole money from me and the two guys in New Orleans that used me and Frankie to steal from all those tourists.

"What were their names, anyway?" I ask Frankie. "That cop told me. Scott, I think was one of them. I can't remember the other one. Those two guys almost got you taken away from me, you know that?"

I get a little sick to my stomach when I think about how close I came to losing her. If he hadn't let me go, if he had taken me to the police station, Frankie would have gone into a shelter somewhere and I'd never have seen her again.

"Now those two guys were real pieces of shit, but the cop was okay. Didn't expect that, but I'm sure glad he was."

Daddy had always told me the police were just out to get people like us, and I guess some of them are. Not that cop in New Orleans, though, and not Deputy Anderson. He was okay, too.

Most folks we've run into have been okay, and some of them, like Gamaliel and Mark, have been great, but Jerry was a real asshole, and so were those three guys in Georgia.

I sure wish I was better at figuring out what kind of person I'm dealing with right off. Daddy took the easy way out, figuring everybody was against him. He sure proved he was right about that, over and over again.

I can't think about this too much without getting mad at Daddy all over again, and then I think about that morning in the barn and what I had to do to fix things. I really don't want to get started on that again, so I try to find something else to focus on.

We're out in the middle of nowhere, so it's not easy to get my mind off that stuff, but after about ten more miles I see a sign on the right side of the road that says For Rent.

"Let's go take a look, Frankie. Might as well start trying to find a place to live besides the back of this truck. This is as good a place as any."

That place turns out to be real fancy, and I don't even call the number on the sign to find out how much the rent is. The next two places we look at are about the same, except bigger and fancier, and too rich for our blood.

I almost miss the next sign, a little over a mile farther down the road. The weeds have grown up around it so it's mostly covered up. I turn into the next driveway and drive back to it. Next to the sign is a gravel road, more like two ruts with more weeds growing up between them. There's no house in sight.

We follow the ruts a little ways, and I'm starting to think it's a sign for renting land instead of a house when we go around a little bend and there's a house about the size of our old one sitting all by itself in a field.

It's in better shape than where I used to live before I met Gamaliel, but that doesn't mean much. The closer we get, though, the more it looks like somebody's kept the place up pretty good.

We lived in a single wide for a long time before we moved to the house just down from Gamaliel's. I lived in Gamaliel's house until Jerry raised so much hell I had to move and then lived in that little place on the grounds of the old folks' home. Since I left there, I've had those few weeks on the road and a month of just kind of farting around before heading up to Virginia. Two nights in a motel and now I'm back in the truck. I've had a couple of months living out of my truck and one thing I know for sure is I don't want to keep doing that.

"Wonder what the rent is on this place?"

Frankie's looking around and acting like she needs to pee, so we get out, and after thinking about it for a second I unhook her, leave the leash on the dashboard and let her run.

I've been around the house once and doing it again, looking in the windows this time, when I hear a car. Frankie's nosing around in the field and I call her to me.

The car pulls up right behind the truck and a guy gets out. He comes right up to me and says, "What are you doing on this property?" He doesn't say it mean, but he sounds pretty serious. Maybe he's the owner.

"I saw a For Rent sign and followed the tracks back here," I say. Then we stand there looking at each other for a minute.

"I just took down the sign. Dad," he says, and stops. After a minute he goes on. "This is, or rather was, his place, his getaway, I guess. He passed on a couple of years ago. We'd had the sign out ever since he got sick and we knew he'd never make it back out here, but it's been months since we've had a renter. There's three of us kids, and we're just about ready to give up on the idea of renting and sell the place."

I don't know what to say. I feel bad about him losing his Dad, and I don't know if I should ask about rent, or if I can see inside, or anything like that. So I don't say anything.

He notices Frankie and takes a step back toward his car. "That your dog?"

I nod. "I thought I'd let her stretch her legs while I was looking around. Her name's Frankie." I scratch her ear and she sits down right next to my foot and kind of leans up against me.

He smiles a little. "We've got dogs at home. Bo and Peep. My kids named them," he says, like he has to explain their names to me. "A couple of Corgis. Both of them together wouldn't be half her size. What kind is she?"

I explain how I got her and he nods. "Good for you. Hate to hear about that happening to puppies, but I know it happens all the time." He sticks out his hand. "Name's Ralph Tomlinson."

"Boone Hammond." We shake hands.

"So, anyway," he says.

I start to tell him I understand about not being able to rent the place, but not being able to just makes me want it more, even though I don't know what the inside is like or how much the rent would be. Guess I'm really tired of not having a place of my own. The only place I've ever lived that was mine is the back of my truck.

Ralph says, "We've just decided on selling, and I don't know how long it will take, or if anybody will even be interested in the house or the land. I might be willing to rent it to you month by month, but you'd have to agree to move out as soon as we get a buyer for the property."

I start to say yes right then, but I remember how Tiny was when he was buying the truck. He didn't act like he was in any big hurry even though he knew he wanted to buy it.

"Well," I say. "I'd like to see the inside first, and I'd have to know how much the rent would be."

He nods. "I understand that. Come on. I've got the keys with me."

Inside it's not as nice a place as Gamaliel's. About as good as the one at the home, but not as big, plus the furniture is pretty worn out.

"It's got power and water," Ralph says. "You'd have to pay the electric. There's no water bill; it's on a well."

I nod. "So how much money are we talking about here?"

"Well, you can see there's no TV here, so it's just lights and appliances. And heat, but as small as this is, the electric shouldn't be much. We're asking $300 a month for rent, and with utilities, the last renter said it was about $375, give or take."

I know I can do that much. I've still got almost all of Gamaliel's money, and I know I'm going to have to get a job of some kind.

When I don't say anything right away Ralph says, "Boone, if it was up to me I'd drop the rent to 250, but that's what we've been charging all along. I really can't change it."

I turn to Frankie. "What do you think, girl? Want to settle in here for a while?"

She's already curled up in the corner of the main room, so I guess that's her answer.

"Well, Ralph, I'd like to take it. I sure would like to not have to move in the middle of winter, though."

"I'd be real surprised if anything happens in the coldest part of the year. Nobody's going to want to look at it in February."

"Okay, then. I'll have to get to a place to use my debit card so I can get you the first month's rent."

"Let's say by the end of the week. Does that give you enough time?"

I nod. "I appreciate that. Are you coming by to pick it up, or do I bring it to you, or what?"

"I'll come by on Friday, about lunchtime."

This time I stick out my hand. He takes it, and then hands me the keys.

"You know if you'd come by an hour later the sign would have been gone."

"I know. Almost didn't see it as it was."

He looks around. "Dad loved this place. He'd come here two or three times a month, just for the peace and quiet. He used to say this was better than any church pew." He wipes his eye with the back of his hand. "I really miss the old guy, even after a couple of years."

All this makes me think about Gamaliel. He was better to me than Daddy by a long shot. If I'd gotten to know him before . . . .

There's no way that would have happened, and I know it. Daddy would never have stood for that.

"You okay, Boone?" Ralph is looking at me kind of funny. "You were a thousand miles away just then."

I shake my head. "Your dad sounds a lot like this old guy I used to know. He died a few years back. Him and me got to be pretty good friends before he died."

I really don't want him to ask about my Daddy, but I can tell he's going to, so I jump in and cut him off.

"My daddy left us a while back, not sure where he is or what kind of shape he's in." Only half of that was a lie.

"Sorry to hear that."

I shrug.

"Well, anyway," he says, and I can see he's real uncomfortable right now, "I'd better get going. I'll let everybody know I got a last-minute renter and that we don't have to worry about anything until at least spring."

"I appreciate that. See you on Friday."

"See you then." And he's gone.

When his car's out of sight I turn to Frankie.

"We got us a place, girl. Let's get moved in."

Chapter Five

After two weeks here I still can't believe that I lucked into this place. I'm back to no TV, but that doesn't bother me. We're far enough off the road that I can let Frankie out without worrying about cars, especially since she's good about staying pretty close to the house. It took me a while to find an ATM so I'd have Ralph his money on time, but I got that done. I still need to go back to my bank and put some of Gamaliel's money in my account, but I've got a little time before I have to do that.

I'm not having much luck finding a job, but that's mainly because I'm not looking all that hard.

But the best thing about this is that it's not home. Back home everybody knew who I was, but they also knew who Daddy was, and most of them figured I was probably just like him. It didn't make much difference what I tried to do, folks pretty much had their minds made up before I had a chance.

I'm finally getting out from under that mean old drunk.

I've thought about calling somebody to let them know I'm okay, but I don't guess anybody would care much. Mark would, and Tiny might, but that's about it. So I haven't called.

"I'll give Mark a call in a day or two," I tell Frankie. "Maybe after I get a job."

I think about going by to see Tiny when I go down to the bank to put some money into my checking account, get one of those gallons of shine I left with him, and maybe that old rifle I found in Gamaliel's shed. But I probably won't do that.

"I've got the shotgun, and I don't even know if that old gun works. Probably blow up in my face."

Frankie thumps her tail a couple of times and looks over at me, then lays her head back down.

"I'm going to take a walk outside," I tell her. "Want to come along?"

Usually she's up and ready as soon as she hears the word "walk," but not this time. I'm about to go out the door when she jumps up and trots over to the window that looks out at the driveway. She's not barking, but she definitely heard something. We go out into the yard.

A pickup comes bouncing into the yard and parks next to mine. There's only one guy in it, but he doesn't get out right away. It looks like he's on his phone. Then he puts his phone away and gets out. He walks up to me and says, "You Boone?"

I nod. "How do you know my name?"

"Randy Goodman," he says, and I'm not sure if that's his name or that's who told him who I am. I don't know any Randy Goodman.

"Didn't recognize the truck, so I called Ralph and he told me you were renting the place for a little while."

I nod again. Then, because I figure I ought to say something, I say, "So you knew Ralph's dad?"

Randy nods, then shakes his head real slow. "I knew him for years. Damn shame. Ever meet him?" He doesn't wait for me to answer. "He was a good guy. Suffered a long time before the Lord took him home. Damn shame," he says again.

I'm not sure why this guy is here. I hope he's not going to start preaching to me.

I don't know exactly how to say this. It's really not my place, Ralph is the owner, but since I'm living here I ought to be able to ask, so I do.

"Was there something you needed?"

Randy looks at me for a long minute and I'm thinking I've pissed him off somehow, but then he smiles and says, "I just need to take a quick look. For the last five years or so they've had an awful time with squirrels moving into the walls and setting up housekeeping. Any knothole is like an open door to them, and they can squeeze into cracks you wouldn't think was possible."

When I don't say anything he says, "I've got a business, actually it's just me, C&R services." He stops for a second. "Stands for catch and release. If you've got animals of some kind living alongside you and you don't like sharing, you can give me a call. I'll catch whatever it is, squirrel, snake, raccoon, skunk, and take them far enough away that they can't find their way back."

He looks around. "So, you hear anything? Noises in the walls, scratching around, stuff like that?"

I can tell he wants to come in and look around, and I really don't want anybody just inviting themselves in. He knows Ralph, though, or he wouldn't have known my name, and if I don't let him look around he'll just come back with Ralph and I won't have a choice.

"No, everything's good here. You want to come in, have a glass of Thunderstorm? I wasn't expecting company. It's a little messy."

Randy smiles again, bigger this time. "I'll pass on the Thunderstorm, Boone, but thanks for asking. If you haven't heard anything I'll just make a circle around the house, see if there's any fresh signs."

Frankie's been watching this whole thing, but she hasn't made a noise or moved from beside me. Randy says, "Nice dog."

I nod. "She sure is. Good company."

He takes a slow walk around the house, looking it up and down. Frankie goes along, but I stay put, and when he gets back to me he says, "Looks okay to me. If you don't need anything done, I'll be on my way." He starts toward his truck and then turns around. "Why don't you let me have your number and I'll call the next time, let you know I'm on my way."

I tell him the number and he says, "Nice meeting you, Boone. See you in a month or two, or you can call Ralph if you need me."

He gets in his truck and backs a little, cuts the wheel, and backs on into the yard. Then he heads out and disappears around the trees.

I look down at Frankie. "Ready for that walk?" She's already heading back inside, though, and is curled up in her corner by the time I step through the door.

I'm sitting on the couch a few days later when the phone rings. I don't get phone calls, so I don't recognize the number and almost don't answer it. It might be something about Hannah, though, so I finally pick it up.

"Hey, Boone, this is Randy. I was at your place about a week ago. I'm a friend of Ralph's."

"Yeah, I remember. You on your way back over here?" I'm thinking that's awful soon. I wonder if I'm about to lose this place already. If they've got somebody wanting to buy it, Ralph would most likely send Randy around to make sure everything about the house looked okay.

"No, no, I told Ralph everything looked good. That's not why I called."

When I don't say anything, he says, "Well, I've got a job I'm doing not too far from where you're living. I know where they're getting in, right up next to the roof, and it sure would go a lot faster if I didn't have to go up and down a ladder every time I needed some tool or other. I was wondering if you'd be willing to help out. I'm thinking it's a two day job to finish it up." He stops, and I wait for him to keep going. I wouldn't mind helping the guy out, but I can't help thinking about McIntyre and how all that blew up on me.

"Course I'd pay you, I usually pay my help ten an hour, but if you've got something else you're doing I understand. I'll keep looking," and it sounds like he's about to hang up.

"Hey, Randy, I wouldn't care to help you out, the thing is, I've only been living here a little while and I've left Frankie alone here for a few hours, but I've never left her all day."

"Frankie's your dog?"

I guess I hadn't told him that. "Yeah."

"Hell, bring her along. If she knows enough to stay out of the way, that is. Can't have her running around all over this lady's yard."

"Okay, then, sure, I can help out for a few days."

"Great, Boone, I appreciate it. It's not that I couldn't do it myself, you know, it'll just be a lot quicker this way."

I nod and then say, "Okay, sounds good."

"I'll swing by tomorrow around nine after I pack up the cages and hardware cloth, and you can follow me to the site."

"Sounds good," I say again. I don't much like talking on the phone. Can't see the person I'm talking to.

"Okay," and he hangs up.

It ends up taking three days, which Randy says happens to him a lot. "I try to estimate a job and it almost always turns out to take longer than I thought."

I tell him it's fine, I've got some time and don't mind helping him out. Compared to what I had to do for McIntyre it's an easy job, but I can see why he wanted the help. The house is two stories high, and what time I'm not waiting for Randy to need something else, I'm going up and down ladders. Turns out heights don't bother me at all.

He's a careful guy, and real picky about cleaning up the job site when he's done. We end up with three squirrels in the big cage he keeps in the bed of his pickup, and he patches most of the holes with the hardware cloth. One he leaves open. "I think there's another one or two living there," he says. "I'll reset the trap and see what happens over the next day or two."

He looks around one more time and says, "I think that's it. Want to go grab a beer?"

When I don't answer right away he says, "I figure you're not 21 yet, but there's a couple of places that don't ask. Of course if you don't want one ..."

"Sounds good, Randy. I'll follow you."

We end up having a couple each and he buys a plate of nachos to go with them. We're at an outside table so I can keep an eye on Frankie.

"This is pretty good," I say. "Thanks, man."

"I appreciate the help," Randy says. He gets another big scoop of cheese and hot peppers on his chip and says, "Think you might be interested in doing some more work for me off and on?"

I don't say anything right away, but off and on is pretty much exactly what I'm looking for. He seems like an okay guy to work for, and I can take Frankie with me if I need to.

"It wouldn't be steady work, you understand, but now and then I get a job that really needs two people."

I take another swig. I'm about halfway through my second beer. It's not an S&S, but it's not bad.

"Sure, I'd be interested in something like that," I say. "All your jobs like this one we just finished?"

He says no, every one of them is different.

"So you take them off somewhere and turn them loose?"

He nods.

"What about the people living around there?"

He laughs. "That would be job security, for sure, but kind of unethical. The place I use is on the border of a state park, thousands of acres with no house to move into."

"How come you don't just kill them?"

He gives me a look.

"It's not like they're doing it on purpose, Boone. They don't know it's a house and they're supposed to stay out. It's just another place to build a nest to them. They don't deserve to die for that."

I can see that, and tell him so.

"Good," he says. "There's plenty of folks out there ready to kill anything that gets in their way. Glad you're not one of them."

I never thought about it that way. To tell the truth, I never much thought about it at all. The only wild animal I can remember having anything to do with me was that rabid raccoon, and I killed it without a second thought.

"I don't know, man, a rabid coon almost got Frankie a while back."

He shakes his head. "That's different. Sick animal like that, already suffering and going to die anyway, it's a mercy to put it down. Besides, it may save some kid's life, you know? Keep the kid from getting bit.

"So, if I come across a job that needs an extra guy, you want me to give you a call?"

I start to tell him absolutely, but I don't know anything about wild animals and I figure it'd take him about a minute to see that I was lying if I pretended I did, so I say, "Tell you the truth, I don't know anything about working with animals."

He sets down his bottle. "Well, I don't know about that. Frankie, that's her name, right?" I nod. "Frankie seems to be doing pretty well, and you know a dog's condition will tell you a lot about the owner. I wouldn't expect you to do a job on your own or anything, but sometimes I can use a hand and if you were willing to learn, I guess I could show you a thing or two."

This is like Gamaliel teaching me how to make shine. I don't want to come off like a little kid, but I would love to be able to do something besides break my back. I saw what that did to Daddy. I try to act cool, but it probably shows.

"I'd like that a lot, Randy. Just call me when you've got something else you need me for."

Chapter Six

He doesn't call me again for another week and
a half, but I don't really care. Frankie and I still
have stuff to do.

I go back down to the bank and get the safety
deposit box, take out a little over a thousand, and
leave the rest. I figure I ought to put most of the
thousand in a bank closer to where I'm living.

Tiny's not home when I call, but he says he'll be
there in about an hour. That gives me time to go
see Mark and let him know what's going on.

Mark is in his office and says he has an hour or
so before he has to be somewhere.

"So, are you back?"

"No, not really. I started to head up to Virginia
to see Raymond and Charlotte," and I tell him
about McIntyre and how that job only lasted two
and a half days.

He gives me a look. "Sound like anybody you know?"

That makes me mad until I remember that's why I come to see Mark. He knows a lot about me, likes me anyway, and tells me the truth when he figures I need to hear it, which is just about all the time. It's hard to stay mad when I knew what I was getting into coming here.

"Yeah, a little."

He looks like he's going to say something else, but he doesn't. After a minute he asks, "Did you get my message about your aunt's call?"

"Yeah, I got it. She was the next message after yours."

Mark sits up. "Really? What did she say?"

"Same old shit, told me what a lousy brother I was being and how wonderful she was to take care of Hannah. Then she said she was going to put Hannah in foster care because she was such a little hellion."

He doesn't say anything for a second.

"Anything else?"

"Well, she got cut off right about then. I guess the phone ran out of room or something." I shrug and keep looking at the floor.

"What did she say when you called her back?"

"I didn't call her back."

Mark lets out a long breath. "You have to call her, Boone, and talk her out of that. A child who has already lost both parents and one brother will no doubt see that as another family member abandoning her. She needs you, Boone. She needs to know she hasn't lost you, too. You're all she's got and, well, she's just a little girl."

Now I'm mad at Claire all over again and getting mad at Mark, too. "You think I don't know that? What the hell am I supposed to do? I just now got a place to live and . . . ."

"You do? Where? Who are you living with?"

I'm starting to wish I hadn't come by to see Mark. I was feeling pretty good about having a place and a job, even if it was just a sometimes kind of job, and he's saying the same kind of stuff Claire was saying. I mean, he's nicer about it and all that, but he's still trying to make me feel guilty because I don't run right up there and save her from the foster home. I was about to tell him that I wanted to go get Hannah as soon as I was settled, and now I don't even want to. I mean, I come here all ready to tell him I'm trying to do the right thing, and he gives me shit for not having done it already.

When I don't answer him he starts in again on Hannah. "Most foster parents are good people, trying their best to do an impossible job with not much help, but even the good ones are no substitute for what you can give her. If you can't talk your aunt out of this very poor decision, you at least have to find out where Hannah ends up so you can stay in touch. She needs that, Boone, and you're the only one who can give it."

I'm on my feet now, and Frankie's getting a little worried. She sees me getting ready to go off on Mark and she knows he's one of the good guys.

"Dammit, Mark, I came in here feeling pretty good and now I feel like shit. You think I don't know what I need to do here? I'm trying, man, I mean, I'm really trying." I'm so mad I'm about to start crying like a little kid.

I feel Frankie's nose on the back of my hand and look down. My hands are all balled up into fists. I make myself open them up, but I can't sit back down yet. I start walking around, even though there's almost no room for that kind of thing.

"Your office is too damn small," I say.

When I look up at Mark he's got a little smile on his face. "Well, I put in a request to take over that little house you lived in, but I haven't heard back yet."

I stop walking. "Yeah, that would work." I take a couple of deep breaths and say, "Sorry I went off like that."

He motions to the chair. "Sit down, Boone. I know you're trying, and I meant no criticism. If, as your aunt says, Hannah is turning into a little hellion, I have no doubt it's because she's so angry she doesn't know what to do. You can understand that, I believe."

I nod.

"I know you do. All right, I promise, nothing more about Hannah. Tell me about this new place you found. Are you sharing it with anyone or is it just you and Frankie?" I'm glad he changed the subject. If he'd kept up about what I'm supposed to be doing I'd have been out the door.

When I tell him how it happened he says, "I think you've been due a bit of good luck. I'm happy for you, and for Frankie. Are you looking for a job yet, or still getting settled?"

So I tell him about Randy. "I don't know if it will end up being anything, but maybe I can learn how to do something besides carry stuff around."

"Well, even if it isn't where you end up, it's a place to start." Mark doesn't seem all that impressed with my new job, which bothers me a little.

"In any case, I'm glad you stopped by to fill me in on everything." He looks at the clock on his desk. "I'd buy you lunch at the cafeteria, but I'm afraid I have to meet with someone in just a couple of minutes."

I'm not the smartest guy around, but I can tell when I'm being told to get lost. I stand up and say, "Come on, Frankie. Let's get out of here."

I can hear Mark saying something about not knowing where my new place is, but I'm not in the mood to tell him. What I want to do is stop by and see Tiny and then head back home. Maybe I'll call Mark later and tell him where the house is.

And maybe I won't. I don't usually feel worse after talking to Mark, but that's exactly what happened this time.

It's this thing with Hannah. He's right about one thing, she's just a kid. If I could help her out I would, but it would be stupid for me to take her away from Claire and move her in with me. Mark didn't need to do that whole thing about how much she needs me and I'm the only one that can help her, blah, blah, blah. I got to get my mind on something else.

When I call Tiny he says he's about fifteen minutes from his house and that I should meet him there. I head over that way, taking my time.

"We're going to see Tiny and Eunuch," I tell Frankie, and she wags her tail. I know she likes Tiny, and she and Eunuch get along great together.

Tiny's just getting out of his truck when I pull into the driveway. It's a brand new one, looks like a custom job. It sits way up high, and there's a winch on the front.

"Nice," I say. "When'd you get that?"

"Remember Mac, the guy who used to own your truck? We never talked to him, just his wife Ruth."

I nod.

"Well, he got his custom truck, kept it for a little while, and decided he didn't like it. I heard about it and made him an offer."

It's one hell of a truck, I can tell just by looking at it. "Why the hell would he let something like this go?"

Tiny shrugs. "Mac's funny that way. He'll get it in his head that he doesn't like something and when that happens he wants it, whatever it is, gone. I got a great deal on it because he wanted it out of his yard. Last I heard he was driving something right off the lot and was happy as a pig in shit."

I just shake my head.

"So, what's going on? I thought you were back on the road."

I tell him about McIntyre and how I went off on him and lost that job, and about finding a place to live, and about Randy and how I helped him out with one of his jobs. "I might be doing some more work for him later."

"How come he doesn't just shoot them?"

I tell him what Randy said, that the animals don't know they're in somebody else's house, and there's no reason to kill them for it.

Tiny laughs that short laugh of his. "That's some kind of bullshit there, man. They're just a bunch of pests. You wouldn't catch an ant and relocate it. You'd just step on it."

I shrug.

"You better watch out, Boone. Next thing you know you'll be a vegetarian and joining one of those save the planet groups."

I grin and say, "If you think next time you do a grill party I'm going to turn down one of your famous half pound hamburgers, you're crazier than I thought you were."

He nods. "That's the spirit. So, have you heard from your New Orleans woman? You know, the one you almost kicked Neil's ass over. The way you were acting that day, I figured y'all had something serious going."

"Hell, Tiny, I'll never hear from Billie again. It was just a thing, you know. Besides, I don't know her number and couldn't find my way back to her place if I tried."

Tiny shrugs. "Probably just as well. I think Neil was way out of line, but mixing the races, you know, it's just not right."

Man, this is turning out to be a bad mistake. First Mark preaching to me about Hannah, and now Tiny's giving me shit about Billie. If we keep talking about this stuff I'm going to end up going off on Tiny like I did Mark, but Tiny won't put up with it.

"Listen, man, on the way down I was thinking about that old rifle, you know, the one I asked you to hold on to?"

He nods. "Yeah, it's standing up in the corner of my room. Haven't had a chance to look at it yet, not really."

"Well, what I was thinking was, I've got the shotgun that Daddy left behind, and it'd take somebody that knows guns to do anything with that rifle. So I think you ought to keep it."

"Are you serious? You know that thing's old. It might be worth a ton of money."

"I don't know anything about that kind of stuff, Tiny. It'd have to be restored, you know, and I can't do it, don't know anybody who can. If I kept it, it would just go downhill worse than it has already, and pretty soon it wouldn't be worth anything to anybody. It's better if you take it."

Tiny's got this real serious look on his face. "On one condition. I'll get it cleaned up and have somebody appraise it. When I find out how much it's worth I'll pay you for it."

"Man, I'm not selling you the rifle. I'm giving it to you."

Tiny shakes his head. "I appreciate that, man, I do, but I wouldn't feel right not at least getting it checked out."

I know how Tiny can get about stuff like this, so I say, "All right, just let me know what you find out. Maybe we can split the money or something."

I swear, everything I try to do, seems like, is just another reason for people to give me a hard time, I can't even give something to my best friend without it turning into an argument.

We sit there for a minute watching the dogs run around the field behind Tiny's house. They play a little rough sometimes, but that only lasts for a minute or two and then they're back racing from one end of the field to the other. Tiny's watching them too, and says, "Looks like they're about to wear each other out. I give them five more minutes and they'll be asleep under the big tree."

I nod. "Frankie sure does like Eunuch."

Tiny grins. "What's not to like? It's not like he's going to try to screw her or anything."

I laugh. "I know I had the same thing done to Frankie, but I got to say, taking a dog's balls just doesn't seem right."

"Boone? Is that you?"

I look over at Tiny. "Tell me your mom wasn't close enough to hear what I just said."

He just raises his hands up shoulder high and says, "We'll know in a second." He's grinning like a fool.

Mrs. Thompson walks over to me and says, "Stand up so I can give you a hug! It's so good to see you again, Boone, you left the cookout so quickly I didn't have time to see how you were doing. You'll stay for lunch, of course. I was just getting it ready. Soup and sandwiches, and you build your own sandwich. What can I get you to drink?"

I look over at Tiny. He shrugs and says, "No sense in fighting it, Boone. You've got a place at the table, and we'll even feed Frankie."

"Of course we'll feed that lovely dog," she says. "And she has such a beautiful name," she looks right at Tiny, and I can tell she still gives him a hard time about Eunuch's name.

"Thanks, ma'am, I'd like some lunch, and ice tea would be just fine with me."

"I'll call you when it's ready," she says. "About five, maybe ten minutes."

The lunch is really good, and I tell Tiny's mom all the stuff that I just told him, about the house and the job and all that. She says, "I'm so glad you have a place of your own, Boone. I worried so much about you and Frankie living out of that truck."

"Yes, ma'am," I say. "It's pretty small, but we don't need much."

"I've heard of people doing the kind of work you're talking about. You be careful and don't get bit," she says. "Some of those wild animals carry rabies and all kinds of nasty diseases."

"I will."

Right now I'm real jealous of Tiny. His mom is treating me like a mom ought to, and the last time I saw Momma she was helping some jerk steal my truck.

She's the one that ought to be helping Hannah, not me. She's the one that sent her up there in the first place.

Chapter Seven

After lunch me and Tiny go back out into the yard so he can show off his truck.

He tells me all about the extras that Mac ordered for the interior and how he got the biggest engine and best transmission he could, and on and on, and I'm thinking if I had this truck I wouldn't need anywhere to live.

"So has it got a bathroom?"

He looks at me for a second and then starts laughing. "No, and no stove, no dishwasher, not even a microwave. It's got damn near everything else, though, plus if I had our house up on wheels I bet I could tow it. This thing is a monster."

When I had that piece of shit Daddy used to drive, I thought the one I've got now was the best thing on the road. Now, parked next to Tiny's new truck, I'm back to where I was before.

That old truck I used to have would never have made the trip I just finished, though. I doubt it would have made it to Morristown. Thinking about heading back home reminds me of one of the reasons I wanted to stop by.

"Hey, Tiny, you drink up all that shine I left with you?"

Tiny looks up. "Damn, Boone, not so loud. No, I didn't drink it all up. Why, you taking some with you?"

I nod. "Thought I might."

"Good. The less I have here the less I have to try to keep hid."

He goes and gets a couple of gallons and we put them in the back of the truck. I throw an old tarp over them and close it back up.

"I appreciate you taking care of that," I say. "Since the fire took out all our stuff this might be the end of our shine making days."

Tiny grins. "It was fun while it lasted, though."

"Damn right."

We spend the next hour or so just talking about this and that, watching the dogs sleep in the shade of the big tree, and before I know it it's the middle of the afternoon.

"I better think about heading back home."

"You sure, man?" Tiny's watching Eunuch, who woke up long enough to see a rabbit out in the field and took off running. Frankie's a little slow, but she's got longer legs and pretty soon they're both all over the field trying to figure out where it went.

"That rabbit's long gone," I say.

Tiny nods. "You know if you hang around a while longer you'll get another free meal."

"I better head on," I say.

Mrs. Thompson opens the back door. "Philip!"

I look around to see who else is here, and then remember that's Tiny's name.

"Over here, Mom," Tiny waves. "I'm trying to talk Boone into staying for supper, but he's about to take off."

She comes out into the back yard. "You left your phone on the kitchen table. When I saw who it was on the caller ID I went ahead and answered it."

She holds the phone out to him. "It's Nancy. She says she's calling you back."

I look at Tiny. He's looking everywhere but at me.

"Guess you'd better get that. We're out of here." I look around for Frankie. "Come on, girl!"

Tiny looks like a trapped animal. His eyes keep moving, but never land on me. Won't look at me. I get Frankie in the cab and get in behind the wheel. I start it up and look around, checking for Eunuch.

That big fancy truck of Tiny's is right behind us. I drop the truck into reverse and sit there for a second.

I can see the look on Tiny's face. He knows what I'm thinking. He takes a step toward me. I take it out of reverse and start toward the road, moving slow. In the rearview mirror I see him go around to the driver's side of his truck, but he doesn't get in. He just stands there, watching me and Frankie pull out on the road.

It takes everything I've got to keep it between the lines and under the speed limit. I've never been this mad at Tiny, and maybe never this mad at anybody.

"That son of a bitch," I say to Frankie. "He let me think he didn't know where Nancy was or how to get in touch with her. If I ever see that shithead again I'll kick his ass back down to his momma's house."

I go on like that until we get to the house, and Frankie lets me, but as soon as I open her door she's out of the truck and headed for the woods. I guess she's had enough of me for a while.

I stand beside the truck, looking at the little house.

"So that's it," I say even though Frankie's off in the woods somewhere taking a break. "I got no reason to go back there now." If all Mark's going to do is preach at me, he can do that over the phone. Tiny lied to me about Nancy, and who knows how long that's been going on. I don't even want to think about that. I've still got Frankie, and I've got a place to live, so the hell with all of them.

My phone starts vibrating in my pocket, but I don't even take it out.

Chapter Eight

Randy calls me a couple of times over the next few weeks, and I get enough money to make the rent payments out of the jobs he can't do on his own. One of them is another two story house, but this time it's a family of raccoons in the attic.

"They're strong and smart," Randy tells me. "I know how they're getting in, but we need to make sure they are all out of there before we close it up." That means crawling around in the insulation and I'm real glad I'm not still living in the back of the truck. It takes a long shower to get most of the insulation off of me, and I only have one long sleeved shirt, so I have to wear that over and over.

The other job is another squirrel invasion. That's what Randy calls it if it's more than three squirrels in the same place. This house has nine at least, and he's not all that sure we got them all.

"Sneaky little bastards," he says with a grin. "It's really hard trying to clear them out of a place because of how devious they are, but you got to respect their ability to survive."

After the squirrel job, we're back at the same place having beer and nachos. Randy looks across the table at me.

"You're a good worker, Boone. I figured you'd get one taste of that attic insulation and I'd never see you again."

I grin at him. "Can't say I liked it much."

"I'd take you on full time if I needed anybody, but this kind of work, you know, it comes and goes. Not nearly steady enough to justify me hiring you or anybody else, for that matter."

"Hell, Randy, you told me that up front. I get it. Tell you the truth, I'm crawling around in about as much insulation as I want to as it is."

He laughs. "I'm going out of town for a couple of weeks, so I won't be calling you until next month at the earliest."

"Where you headed?"

"Just on a little trip. I'll be back in a couple of weeks and give you a call when I get another two man job."

I nod. Guess he's not going to tell me.

We finish off our first beers and Randy orders two more and some more queso dip.

"You got family, Boone?"

He's never asked before and I'm not sure why it's coming up now. I shake my head.

"No, no family. What about you?"

"My folks are up in Ohio. I got one brother, Danny, he lives close to them and helps out. They're getting on in years. My sister Rachel moved out to Montana six or seven years ago. She comes in for holidays."

I nod.

He's quiet for a minute. "So, what happened to your family?"

I tell him Momma and Daddy fought all the time, and one day Momma and my sister went to live with my aunt. I just came home to an empty house. That's not how it happened at all, but I'm not about to tell him anything close to the real story. I haven't even told Mark the whole truth.

"Don't know where Daddy is."

"Man, that's rough."

I don't say anything. I'm hoping he gets the idea that I really don't want to talk about this.

He dips a chip into the queso. "Just one sister then? What's her name?"

"Hannah. I had a brother, but he died a few years back."

He shakes his head. "Man, I'm sorry. What was his name?"

"Frankie."

He looks at me, and then at the truck where Frankie's sitting in the passenger seat waiting for me to take her home.

"I wondered why you had a female dog named Frankie. I get it now. That's nice, naming her after your brother."

"Yeah."

I mean, I like Randy and all that, but I really don't want to talk about this stuff. I'm starting to think I'm just going to have to get up and leave, but he beats me to it.

"Listen, Boone, I need to get home and start packing."

"No problem." I'm already on my feet and then I think maybe I ought to pay this time. Randy took care of it the last time, wouldn't let me give him anything, so I pull out my wallet. Randy shakes his head.

"I got this, Boone. It's not like I pay you enough to treat me to beer and nachos." He grins.

I remember from the Cafe du Monde in New Orleans that we're supposed to leave some kind of tip, so I say, "Well, let me get the tip, then."

"Okay," he says, "but don't give them too much or they'll expect it every time."

"So what do you think?"

"Five at the most."

I pull out a five dollar bill and stick it under a plate.

"Thanks for the beers. You have a good trip."

Randy nods. "Take care, Boone. I'll call you when I get back in town."

He waves at Frankie and heads off toward his truck.

I get in next to Frankie and say, "I'm kind of glad he's going out of town, girl. He's an okay guy but that attic job was nasty."

With Randy gone there's not much of anything I have to do, which suits me just fine. Frankie won't let me sleep too late, and we spend some time checking out the area right around the little house. It's not too different from what I'm used to, except there's no stream running through it.

I could see living here for a while, but I know I can't count on that, since Ralph and his family are still planning to sell it.

"Wonder how much they'd want for this," I say to Frankie on one of our walks. "Not that it makes any difference. There's no way I could afford to buy a place." I kept from using too much of the money Gamaliel left me for rent while Randy had a job for me every now and then, but I figure with winter coming on that's not going to last. I don't know much about buying houses and land, but I do know that what I've got wouldn't do it.

About a week after Randy took off I'm sitting out on the tailgate, sipping an S&S and watching the sunset, when my phone lights up. It's a number I don't recognize. I've been pretty much ignoring my phone ever since that day at Tiny's, not that I get that many calls. Randy had called a couple of times to get me to help him on those jobs, and I got one from Ralph just checking on how I was settling in. I would answer if Mark called, but he hasn't. I can't think of anybody else I'd be interested in talking to.

Except Hannah. I'd talk to her.

I'd call her except I really don't want to have to talk to Aunt Claire. When she gets me on the phone all she does is tell me what a worthless brother I am and how Momma has been a real disappointment, and on and on and on. So the only way to talk to Hannah is to go through Claire, and I just can't make myself do that.

This time I decide to answer. I hit the button, put the phone up to my ear, and say hello.

"Hey, Boone, it's Randy. I was afraid you wouldn't pick up if you didn't recognize the number, but I'm glad you did."

He's quiet for a minute. I've already said hello, so I just wait for him to go on.

"Listen, I wanted to let you know that things have changed. I know I told you I'd be back there before too long, but the way it's turning out, I'm not going to be back at all. Mom's real sick and Dad's too proud to ask for help, so my brother and I are going to have to stay real close by. We don't think it's going to be too long before he comes up against something he can't handle, and I can't be a couple of hundred miles away when that happens."

"So you're moving?" It's a stupid thing to say, I realize that as soon as it's out of my mouth.

"Actually I've already kind of settled in up here. I could tell as soon as I got here and talked to Dad that I really didn't have much choice. I'll be back down to clear out my house and put it on the market, but, yeah, I'm moving up here. So that means no more crawling around in insulation for you, buddy."

"That wasn't so bad."

I keep right on saying stupid stuff because I can't think of anything else to say. Working for Randy didn't bring in hardly any money, but then it wasn't really hard work either.

Randy laughs. "That's some real bullshit there, Boone." Somebody else in the room says something and he says, "Listen, I got to go. You take care of yourself and Frankie, Boone."

"You, too," I say, and he hangs up.

"Well, that's that," I say to Frankie. "Guess I'll have to look for something else. I kind of liked just working every now and then."

A couple of days later the phone rings again and I answer it, thinking maybe it's Randy again, looking to unload some of those cages. Not that I'd have any idea about how to do anything besides follow him around and take orders.

I wouldn't mind that kind of job, though. Most of the time it's outside, and you don't have to deal with people hardly at all. Plus there were all those days off in between jobs. I kind of liked that too. I figure if it's him I'll offer to buy his stuff from him and see what happens. So I say hello.

This time it isn't Randy, and I wish I'd just let it ring.

83

Chapter Nine

"Boone?"

Just hearing her voice makes me so mad I can't even answer.

"Boone? Is that you?"

"Yeah."

"Please don't hang up. Okay?"

I'm standing in the front door looking out at my truck, and I don't know what to say.

"Okay?"

"What do you want, Nancy?"

"Tiny told me you were there when I called. I'm so sorry, Boone, I meant to call you. I mean . . ."

She kind of trails off, and we're both breathing into the phone. I'm waiting for her to finish whatever it was she was saying and finally she says, "Damn it, Boone, you're not making this any easier."

"Did you call to tell me about you and Tiny? I kind of figured that out already."

I really thought I was over her until right now.

"There isn't anything between me and Tiny. That's what I'm trying to tell you. I've been calling him to find out, I mean to make sure you're okay."

"Is that right?"

"That's right. We were, I mean, we're both worried about you."

I'm walking back and forth in the yard. Frankie comes up and starts walking with me, right up next to me. I take a real deep breath.

"So you and him are so worried that you've been talking, and whatever, and neither one of you told me? Nobody asked me if I was okay. If you wanted so bad to know how I was doing, how come you threw away that note I sent you? It had my number on it and everything."

"What note?"

"The note I gave Tiny to give you when Stan wouldn't let me anywhere near you."

After a second she says, "I, uh, I don't think he ever gave me a note from you, Boone."

She's lying. Damn, I thought I was mad before.

"Okay, listen. Either you're lying to me, Tiny's lying to me, or both of you are. Why don't you get back together with him and get your stories straight and call me back. Or don't. I don't much care."

It takes two or three punches to turn the damn phone off, and I've got my arm back to throw it up against the wall of the house but then I just let my arm drop. I'm getting so damn tired of being so damn mad.

"Come on, Frankie," I say. "Let's go for a ride." She's on her way to her side of the truck already, and I go back in to get the keys. I set the phone on the kitchen counter and walk out the door.

A couple of days later the stupid thing goes off again. When I look at it, it's another number I don't recognize. I figure, what the hell, it can't get any worse than it is right now, so I answer.

"Hello, I'm looking for Boone Hammond. Ralph gave me this number. Is this Boone?"

"That's right." I don't have any idea who this is or what this is about.

"Ralph told me that you have a pickup truck and might have time to do a little work for me."

It's only been a week since Randy called me, but I'm wondering if Ralph knows about him moving and wants to make sure he gets his rent money.

"What kind of work are you needing done?"

"It's just a couple of days, maybe not even that, and if you're already busy I can find somebody else." This woman sounds like she's probably eighty years old.

"I might have some time, ma'am. What kind of work is it you need done?"

I'm repeating myself, but I had to do that a lot at the home, so I'm kind of used to it.

"Well, it's a couple of things, really. Thirty years ago when Bobby and I moved here we planted a rosebush, and it's so big and overgrown and with him gone now I just want it out of there. I've got some tools, but they're old, and Bobby was too laid up to use them the last eight or ten years, so if you have your own, you know, I just want it cut down, all the way to the ground, and hauled off.

"The other thing is, I've got two dogs, and they both need their yearly trip to the veterinarian, and I don't get out on the road unless I just have to, you understand, so they need a trip to get their shots and a checkup. They're nice dogs, and I have a carrier so they'd be no trouble. Ralph said you have a dog, Is that right?"

"Yes, ma'am."

We talk for another couple of minutes and I get directions to her place. It's about six miles back up toward Virginia, still on 11W.

"Hey, Frankie, let's go check out this rosebush."

Turns out it's more like a hedge than a bush. Damn thing must stretch twenty feet along the side of her driveway. I can see why she wants it gone. It's growing out into the driveway and the branches drag along the side of the truck as I pull up to her house.

I leave Frankie in the car and go up to the house to meet this old woman. The person who answers the door is definitely not old.

"You must be Boone," she says. "Come on in."

She turns and wheels into the hallway. I follow her in, looking around at the house.

It's set up for her, I can tell. Every room I pass has lots of open space, and some things are on low shelves, I guess so she can reach them.

Up to now the only people in wheelchairs I've been around were at the home, and those folks were all real old. One kid at school had to be in one, but we never saw him. I think he had classes in some other part of the school. I remember he had people carrying his lunch tray for him and there was this one girl who was always with him, getting stuff for him and things like that, like maybe that was her job. Course I only saw them a few times, so I don't really know.

"We're back here, Boone," I hear the same voice I heard on the phone, the old woman. Down at the end of the hall I can see a big kitchen, and a table up next to the window.

I can hear the dogs before I see them. About a second later they come through the doorway and head straight for me, barking their heads off. They look like that little dog in *The Wizard of Oz*. That was Hannah's favorite movie. Every time it was on the TV she'd be in front of it, and Momma had an awful time getting her to eat or go to bed or anything else.

"I see you've met Bert and Ray," the old woman says when I finally make it into the kitchen. "They make a ferocious racket, but they won't bite you. What kind of dog do you have?"

I tell them about how I got Frankie and the old woman says, "I had a good feeling about you from the start, young man. I told Molly so as soon as I hung up the phone."

"Frankie's a great dog," I say. "She goes where I go, so I hope it won't be a problem if I bring her along while I'm working."

The old woman says, "I would love to meet your Frankie. I don't suppose you brought her with you today."

"She's in the truck. I don't take her anywhere she might have to spend any time in there, but I thought I could get her out on her leash while I'm looking at the roses. She's real good about staying next to the truck while I'm working on something."

"I think you should bring her in so she can meet Bert and Ray," she says. "I was just about to suggest a cup of tea, or coffee if you prefer that. Why don't you go get her and bring her inside?"

I look over at Molly. She shrugs. "If Gram says bring her in, you might as well. I'll go with you in case you need some help."

My first thought is what could you do to help, but I've got enough sense not to say it. "Sure," I say. "Let's go."

"I can't do much except get the front door," Molly says while we're heading back down the hallway.

"You're fine," I say. "Let me get Frankie and we'll be right back up here."

She's got the door open when we get back up there and Frankie spends a good minute sniffing all around the wheelchair.

"Sorry," I say. "It's not like she's never seen one before. Guess she's just curious."

Molly waves her hand. "I don't mind. She seems to be a great dog. Frankie's kind of a funny name, though. One of these days you can tell me that story, but right now we ought to introduce her to Gram and the boys."

Frankie is a big hit with Gram, whose name is Sylvia Wallsmith. She tells me I have to call her Sylvia so she won't feel like she's a hundred years old.

At first Bert and Ray are pretty skittish around Frankie, but since it's their house they settle down all right.

"Boone, would you like a cup of tea? Or coffee?"

"Coffee would be nice, ma'am, I mean Sylvia."

"Would you like cream? Sugar? A drop of brandy?"

"Gram!" says Molly. "It's 10:30 in the morning!"

Sylvia shakes her head. "Molly's too worried about me, Boone. Dear, I did say a drop. I'm not going to turn up the bottle."

"Black is fine, Sylvia, thanks."

She shakes her head, but pours the coffee and we sit around the table looking out over the back yard. Frankie is curled up right at my feet.

"So, Boone, when can you start?"

"I'd like to have a look at the roses before I leave, but I can start day after tomorrow if that's all right."

She nods and I say, "Is there somewhere you want me to haul them to?"

Sylvia nods again. "I know a gentleman who has a good-sized farm not far from here. He has a gully that he's trying to fill with whatever he can find to slow down the erosion, and said he'd be glad to take it as long as he didn't have to handle the bushes himself."

I finish the coffee and say, "Thanks. I'd better get going. If you'll tell me where those tools are I'd like to take a look at them before I take off."

She turns to Molly. "Dear, would you show Boone where Bobby's tools are?"

"Sure thing, Gram. Come on, Boone."

She wheels out of the kitchen and down a ramp to the driveway. There's a garage about fifteen feet behind the house.

"They're all in there," she points. "Not in the best shape, I'm afraid."

"That's okay. Just need to know what to bring with me when I get ready to work." I look over at her. "You live here with Sylvia?"

She looks up at me with a little smile. "Why? You wondering if I'll be here when you come back?"

My face gets red, and I say, "Well, I guess. I mean, sure. Besides, somebody's got to keep the brandy away from Sylvia."

For a second there I'm sure I just said the worst thing I could have said, and I figure I'm about to get fired again, this time before I even start.

Molly stares at me for what seems like a long time and then starts laughing. "You should see your face right now, Boone!"

I grin. "I'll bet. Soon as I said that I figured I'd screwed up something awful."

She's still laughing. When she stops she says, "You might want to wait until you get to know Gram a little better before you try that kind of thing on her."

"Definitely. So, I'm going to look these tools over and get out of here before I say something else stupid."

"Okay," she says and whirls the chair around. "See you day after tomorrow."

Bobby's tools are in okay shape, so I pick up some WD-40 to clean them up some and a pair of heavy gloves. I figure I'll need those for the roses.

When we're at home I take all the stuff that is still in the bed of the truck inside the house and slide the camper top off into the yard next to the back door.

"I'll not be able to get that back on without some help," I say to Frankie when I get back in the kitchen. She's been watching all this from inside the house where I put her so I wouldn't worry about having to watch for her.

Compared to working for McIntyre, this is not bad at all. Once I get a little ways into the roses, I can reach down to ground level and chop them off. The jacket I got at the thrift store when the weather started cooling off keeps me from getting all scratched up, and I'm sure glad I bought those gloves. I get a little over half of the bushes cut, loaded into the truck, and hauled off to the gully on the first day.

Sylvia's paying me fifteen an hour, which is more than I've ever made before anywhere and I think is way too much, but she says they remind her of Bobby and she'll be so glad to see them gone she's glad to pay it.

Molly comes out twice that first day. Once as soon as I get there, before I even get started, she rolls up with a thermos of coffee.

"Mind if I join you?"

"I don't know," I say. "What's in the coffee?"

She smiles. "Nothing, Boone, not even milk and sugar. Straight black, just like you had it before."

She doesn't stay long. About lunchtime she's back, but she's empty-handed.

"Sylvia says sandwiches will be ready in about fifteen minutes. You drink coffee for lunch?"

"Nope. Iced tea, or Thunderstorm, or water, or whatever you two are having will be just fine."

Molly makes a face. "That Thunderstorm stuff is nasty. Way too much caffeine for me."

You've never had it with a little shine mixed in, I think, but what I say is, "Either tea or water is good. Tell Sylvia thanks and I'll be up as soon as I get this one bush cut and into the truck."

"I'll wait," she says. "Maybe I'll go hang out with Frankie. I'm sure she's got some stories to tell."

I grin at her. "You have no idea."

Chapter Ten

Sylvia feeds me lunch both days, and that second afternoon when it's time to take Bert and Ray to the vets, she says, "If you have room, I'd like for Molly to ride along. The vets know her. And it may make Bert and Ray feel a little better."

I think about the cab of my truck. The carriers for Bert and Ray should fit behind the seat, and Molly's chair could go in the bed of the truck.

"Sure, if you don't mind Frankie riding up front with us."

"Sounds like fun."

It's pretty cramped, even with the carriers on the little seats in the space behind the front seat. "Frankie likes the window," I tell Molly, "so you might have to take the middle."

I'm a little worried about how to get her into the truck, but she wheels around to the passenger side and waits for me to open it. She gets her chair up as close as she can to the seat and says, "It's a little high. Can you help me in?"

I stand there like an idiot and she laughs. "Just pick me up, Boone, I'm not that heavy. I'd haul myself in, but your truck sits up too high."

She backs up a little to give me some room and locks the wheels. I get my arms behind her back and under her legs and lift her into the truck, thinking I'm about as clumsy at this as I have ever been at anything.

"Don't be embarrassed, Boone. I'm not shy about asking for help when I need it. You did fine."

"Thanks. Never done that before."

"Well, they say you never forget your first time." She winks at me. "Put the chair in the back, and I'll scoot over and make room for Frankie."

It's pretty crowded, but Molly doesn't seem to mind. I sure don't, and Frankie is, well, kind of putting up with it. Ray and Bert are used to riding in their carriers, so for them it's no big deal.

The vet trip takes about half the afternoon, and when we get back and unpack all the people and animals, Molly gets settled into her chair and looks up at me.

"How old are you, Boone?"

When I tell her she shakes her head.

"Not quite twenty-one, so you can't take me out for a beer, right?"

I shrug. "Guess not." I look down at the ground and over at the truck. Frankie's waiting on me. "I'd like to, but I can't do it. Sorry."

She reaches into a pocket on the side of her chair. "Fortunately, I turned twenty-one a couple of months ago, so I can take you. If you're interested, that is."

I look at her.

"I know, what's a girl in a wheelchair doing with a driver's license?" She puts it back in the pocket. "For one thing, it's the kind of ID everybody asks for. For another thing, there's a guy over in Middle Tennessee that does conversion jobs on cars, vans, whatever, to set up hand controls. One of these days I'll get one."

I finally get over being surprised enough to say something. "A beer would be great. There's a place that's not real big on checking IDs."

When I tell her the place she nods. "I know where you're talking about. It'd be a lot better if one of us was legal, in case they have a new staff member or a surprise inspection. If they're being picky, we might have to buy one beer at a time and split it." She grins at me. "Tomorrow night work for you?" When I nod she says, "Come on. You've got to get paid, we need to get Bert and Ray out of these carriers and tell Gram how it went, and I'll let her know I've got a date."

Sylvia waits until Molly is out of the room and turns to me. "Thank you, Boone."

I haven't done anything she ought to be saying thanks for, and I tell her that.

She shakes her head. "Molly, well, most people just see the chair. I've watched you, Boone, you don't look down on her."

"Yes he does, Gram," Molly is in the doorway. "It's okay though, everybody does. I'm down here, remember?"

I don't know what to say, but when I look at her she's smiling, and so is Sylvia.

"Anyway," I say. "See you tomorrow."

"Around 6:30," she says. "Don't be late."

I leave Frankie with a bowl of food, pick Molly up, and we head over to the restaurant. It's not crowded at all, and I say, "Why don't we eat out on the patio?"

She hesitates and finally says, "It's hard for me to get out there, and if I have to go to the bathroom it's a real hassle. If you don't mind, I'd like to eat inside. There's a table I usually get."

There's one table off to the side right next to the swinging doors the servers go in and out of all the time that has a little sign that says "Handicapped Accessible."

"It's the only one in this restaurant," Molly says.

"We can go somewhere else," I say, and she shakes her head.

"They're all like this," she says, "unless they don't have one at all and have to make do when I show up. Those places hate to see me coming."

"That sucks," I say.

"Tell me about it," she says. "Let's talk about something else, like how Frankie got her name."

So I tell her about my brother and she asks me about the rest of my family. I tell her the same lies I tell everybody, and when I finish she says, "I'm so sorry, Boone, that must be awful."

"It was a long time ago," I say. "So what about you? You live with Sylvia long?"

She tells me her story, about Sylvia's daughter and her husband divorcing and how she ended up at her Gram's house.

"It's a great place to live," she says, and it's the first time I've seen her smile since we got here. "I couldn't ask for better."

After that we stay away from family stuff. I tell her some about my road trip and she says, "I knew you'd have some great stories. I'd love to go on a trip like that sometime."

"I'll let you know when I'm ready to hit the road again," I say before I think about it.

"Sorry," I say. "I don't even really know you yet."

"Well," she says, and when I look up she's got a funny look on her face, "that would sure be a way to get to know each other better."

I don't even know what to say to that, so I look around for the waiter. "I think I need another beer."

She shakes her head. "No, you don't. You're driving, remember? Let's finish this food and go for a drive. We can go check on Frankie."

"I can't take you there," I say.

"Why not?"

I point to the sign. "It's not handicapped accessible. Give me time to build a ramp and I'll give you the grand tour. All five rooms."

"Oh. Good," she says. "I was afraid you had a wife and kids or something like that."

I laugh. "Hell, Molly, I'm not old enough for anything like that."

She shakes her head. "One of the guys I went to high school with, same grade, is married with two kids already. It happens."

"Well, anyway, I promise to show it to you real soon."

I don't think I've ever just gone for a drive with a girl before. It's a clear night and we spend a good hour just driving around and talking. Molly knows the back roads, so we don't end up back on 11W until we're close to Sylvia's house.

When we pull in she turns to me and says, "It's a lot easier to do this here than after I get back in the chair," and leans over and kisses me. It lasts long enough to be a really good kiss.

"Wow," I say when she leans back.

She's just sitting there smiling at me. I scoot over to her and this one's just as good, maybe better.

"I need to go talk to Gram," she says. I figure I must have done something wrong, but I'll be damned if I know what it was. I start to apologize and she says, "I'm sure we are going to have to call you back out here for some more work. I just don't know what it is yet."

I start laughing, and so does she, and I reach over and pat her on the leg before I even think about what I'm doing. I jerk my hand back, and reach for the door handle. "Sorry," I say.

"I didn't mind," she says.

It takes me a second to get the chair out and bring it around to her side of the truck. When I reach in and pick her up she wraps her arms around my neck and gives me another kiss, and I stand there, holding her in my arms, until I'm afraid I'm going to drop her. I set her down in the chair and take a deep breath.

"See?" she says. "I told you it would get easier."

I must have looked puzzled because she says, "You know, the getting into and out of the truck."

I nod. "Right. Easier."

She touches my lips with the tips of her fingers. "That gets easier, too."

I nod. "It sure does."

When I tell the guy at the lumberyard the next day that I need to build a wheelchair ramp, he gives me all kinds of bullshit about ADA specs and how wide it has to be and how much weight it has to hold and on and on. I just buy enough lumber to build a 12' ramp and go back to the house. When I get there I stand back and look at it, trying to figure out how to make this work.

The ground slopes up a little to the right of the house. If I put the ramp over there it won't have to be nearly as steep, since the ground is just about a foot below the side of the porch. I'd have to park on that side of the house or push Molly around there, but I can do that, I think.

When I get done I bounce up and down on it a couple of times. It's ugly as sin, but it seems pretty sturdy, and I only spent about half of what Sylvia paid me to clear out her roses.

It's three or four days before my phone rings again. When I say hello, Ralph says, "I understand you've done some work on the place."

Oh, hell. I didn't even think about asking for permission to build the ramp. I hate the thought of tearing it down, wasting all that money, but I'm afraid I'm going to have to.

"Yeah, I just put in a ramp the other day. I can tear it out, won't take any time at all."

"That's not what I'm calling about, although the next time I need to know before you start if you want to do something to the place."

"I will, Ralph, I should have this time. Sorry about that."

"Well, don't tear it out. Sylvia has been a friend of the family for a long time, and we all love Molly. I'm assuming that's who the ramp is for."

"Right."

"She's a good kid, Boone. You treat her right, understand?"

I nod, and then say, "I will."

This feels like the kind of talk I'd be having with Molly's dad if he was still around. I'm starting to wonder why he's so interested in me and Molly when he starts talking again.

"Okay, now that that's settled. Sylvia says you did a good job on that awful mess of a rosebush."

"I'm glad she was satisfied."

"I was wondering if I could give your name to one or two other people I know who need jobs done. They'd be small jobs, you understand, and mostly just muscle work. Kind of like what you did for Sylvia."

"Sure, that'd be fine. I appreciate you giving me a heads up, so I'll know the calls are coming."

There's a long silence, and I'm thinking we've gotten disconnected, when Ralph laughs a little and says, "Okay, I get it. You didn't call me about the ramp, and I didn't call you about giving your name to Sylvia. Neither one of us is going to do that again, though. Right?" He pauses again and then says, "I should have checked with you before giving your number out like that. Guess we're even now."

I hadn't even thought about it that way, and I'm about to say so when Ralph says, "Listen, I've got somebody coming into the office in about a minute, so I'll talk to you later." He hangs up before I can say anything else.

I fix a sandwich for lunch and take it out into the yard. Frankie gets about a third of it, as usual, and I make sure her water dish is full when I go back into the kitchen. I mix an S&S and go back outside, jump up and down on the ramp a couple more times, and think about Ralph's call.

This might work out okay, even without Randy and his wild animal business. If Sylvia and Ralph both like that little job I did, maybe I'll get one or two jobs a month and not have to use up Gamaliel's money so fast. I can always say no if I don't feel like hauling trash or whatever, and I won't have to put up with people like McIntyre or those jerks that Daddy worked for all those years. Even if I do it'll only be for a day or so.

The next job I get is from somebody Sylvia told about me, and it's, like Ralph said, just muscle work. This guy has a storage shed he wants to make into a studio for his wife, whatever that is, and he just wants all the stuff gone.

"You want this all to go to the dump? If I find something you might want to keep, you want me to set it off somewhere so you can look at it?"

He says no, he doesn't want any of it. "I've got too much stuff already. Take it to the dump, take it to your house, burn it, I don't care. I don't guess you do finish carpentry, do you?"

"No, never done any finish work."

"Too bad. It's going to need some rough-in work when it's cleaned out, but Marjorie wants that south wall to have a couple of windows to let in light and a nice place to do her painting. You know anybody I can call to do that kind of thing?" I tell him I'm new in town and can't help him out.

It takes three days to clean it out and haul the stuff away. He pays me fifteen an hour, same as Sylvia did, but what I get out of that shed is as good as getting paid a lot more.

Chapter Eleven

There's a lot in here that really is junk, bags of old clothes, stuff like that. I've already taken off one truckload and I'm trying to decide if I can get in one more run before the end of the day when I find a tool chest, one of those big things on wheels with drawers. I forget about making one more dump run and load the box into the bed of the truck.

When I get it home I park next to the ramp and roll it into the house. It takes the rest of the only roll of paper towels I've got just to get the outside cleaned up. No telling how long that thing's been in there.

Some of the drawers up top just have a bunch of old rusted washers and screws, and I leave them where they are. I can take the drawers out the next time I go to the dump and just throw all that old rusty crap away. I find some stuff in the bottom two drawers, the deep ones, that reminds me a lot of Gamaliel.

His shed had some hand tools in it that I spent a little time cleaning up when I was watching the place for him, and the ones in this tool chest are a lot nicer than those. There's only one saw and it's rusted all to hell, but the hammers, clamps, chisels, and screwdrivers are all in good enough shape that I can clean them up.

So I get a pretty good set of tools and a big tool chest to keep them in. All I need to do now is learn how to use them.

The next day I get most of the shed emptied and the only other thing I find is a cardboard box full of books. I look inside and they look like they're still in pretty good shape, so I take them home, too.

The guy gives me an extra ten because I borrow a broom from him and get the place all swept out before I take off with the last load.

"Looks good," he says. "Or, I should say, it will look good when I get it finished out. Nice work, Boone, thanks."

About a week later I hear from Sylvia.

"Molly has been looking around and has a list of jobs for you, Boone," she says. "I'm not sure how urgent these jobs are, but if your schedule isn't full, maybe you could give us a day or two."

"I'd be glad to, Sylvia. I'd like to see Molly again anyway. I've, I've kind of got a surprise for her."

"Really?" Sylvia sounds curious. "I can't wait to see this."

"I can come by tomorrow, middle of the morning, and take a look at the list."

The next morning about ten I pull up next to the house and Molly opens the door.

"So what is this surprise?"

"I knew I shouldn't have told Sylvia about that. Let me take a look at your list, and then I'll show it to you."

"That's not fair," she says, but heads back to the kitchen. "Gram is back here."

"Good morning, Boone. Coffee?"

"Thanks, Sylvia." I take the cup and sit down.

Molly rolls up next to me and Sylvia hands me the list before she sits down. I take a quick look, and it's a lot of landscaping kind of work, nothing that looks too hard.

"Yeah, I can take care of this later on this week," I say. I turn to Molly. "If you're not busy, you want to take a ride?"

"So where are we going?"

"Well, before we go anywhere I want to check on Frankie," I say, pulling out of the driveway and heading toward my house.

"I see. Think she's torn up the house or something?" I look over at Molly and she's got a little smile on her face. I think about what Sylvia said to me about people looking at Molly and just seeing the chair. I don't know what that's like, but I do know what it's like to have people look at me and not even see me. For me that's most of the time, and usually I don't mind, but sometimes I do. And if they do notice me they don't see anybody they want to bother getting to know, so I guess I sort of know what she has to put up with.

I remember at that restaurant when Mark got treated like he wasn't even there by that stupid bitch of a waitress. When I said that was kind of like how people treated me he set me straight right away. Said it wasn't the same at all, that being black is real different. So I guess I ought to be careful about thinking I know what it's like to be where Molly is, since I've never been there.

She doesn't see the ramp right away. I didn't put in handrails or anything like that, so unless you know it's there it's kind of hard to see.

"This is nice," she says, looking around. "Frankie inside?"

I nod. "Let's go check on her."

I get out and bring her chair around before she has a chance to say anything. When I open the door she scoots over and I pick her up and put her in her chair. It's a little rough going through the yard, but I manage to get her up to the ramp.

"I'll work on smoothing that part of the yard," I say. "Ready to test this out?"

When we get to the porch I say, "Ugly as sin, but it's sturdy. Maybe it needs a coat of paint."

She's looking straight ahead and reaches back with one hand, waving it around until I grab hold of it. She squeezes it and then eases up, but she doesn't let go.

Her voice is really low, like a whisper. "That's maybe the best surprise I've ever gotten. In my life."

I don't know what to say to that. I don't get the chance to surprise anybody very often, so I don't know if I'm supposed to make a big deal out of it or not.

"Let's see if Frankie's torn the place up," I say.

She lets go of my hand. "In a minute," she says. I want to try out the ramp on my own." She spins around and says, "Out of my way, Boone. I'll be back in a second."

It's pretty clear by the time she makes it back to the porch that I need to clear out the area at the edge of the ramp. It's rough enough that she has a hard time making the turn to come back, but she does it, and when she gets back to the porch she's got a huge smile on her face.

"Ugly as sin, but sturdy," she says, and laughs out loud. "I love it! Does Gram know about this?"

"Not unless Ralph told her," I say. "I almost got in trouble for building this without checking with him first. It's his house, you know."

"Oh, Ralph," she says. "He's fine. A little loud sometimes, but Gram and I love the whole family to death."

We stand there for a minute without saying a word, her smiling up at me and me not knowing what the hell to do or say.

Finally I say, "We'd better check on Frankie, and I told you I'd give you a tour of the whole house. Should take no time at all." I had picked up some of the stuff lying around before I went over to Sylvia's, but I bet anybody coming in for the first time would think it was a real mess.

I look back at the ramp. "I think I'll add some kind of railing so you don't drive off the side."

Molly turns to look at it. "Okay, but I think it's wide enough that I won't. It's great, Boone, really great." She reaches up and pulls me into a thank you kiss, one that I'm real sorry to have end.

Frankie is sitting by the couch when I open the door. She trots straight over to Molly and stands beside her, wagging her tail.

"Looks like she's glad to see you," I say.

"It's mutual," Molly scratches Frankie behind the ear. "How are you, you beautiful girl?"

I give Molly the grand tour, which really does take about a minute. She doesn't say anything about the tool chest in the middle of the living room, but she does about the box of books.

"Where did these come from?"

"Same place as the tool chest. A guy hired me to clear out a shed and said to throw away or take home whatever was in there."

"You a reader, Boone?"

"Not really. Just didn't feel right throwing them out. They looked like they were in okay shape."

"Well, I am. A reader, I mean. You'll have to let me look through these sometime, see if there's any titles I haven't heard of." She looks up at me. "That's me asking for an invitation to come back."

"Sure," I say. "I've got this ramp and all."

Before I know it Molly's been here for over an hour and we've spent it just talking about nothing in particular. It reminds me of those times me and Gamaliel would sit and talk about this and that and before we knew it the afternoon was gone. Of course with Gamaliel I wasn't thinking about sex.

I don't even know if somebody who has to use a wheelchair can have sex. I like Molly a lot, and I think she's really pretty, she's easy to talk to, and a great kisser, but I don't even know how to think about doing anything else with her.

"Boone? Are you in there somewhere?"

Molly's looking at me, and so is Frankie.

"Yeah, sorry," I say.

"What in the world were you thinking about?"

"Nothing."

She starts laughing and it's a half a minute before she can stop long enough to say, "You are red as a beet, Boone!" She shakes her finger at me. "I bet I know what's on your mind!"

I can't even look at her.

"What you need is a distraction," she says, still laughing. "Or a cold shower."

I don't understand what's going on here. She's laughing at me, and I'd swear Frankie is too, and I'm not mad about it. Usually I'd be ready to pick a fight or at least get all pissed off, but I'm not, and I don't know exactly why. I'm just trying to think of something to say that's not really stupid.

"I don't want a cold shower. What was my other choice again?"

Molly stops laughing long enough to say, "Distraction," and then is about to start again. She takes a deep breath instead, and says, "It feels so damn good to have something to laugh about. It cleans out your soul, did you know that?"

I don't have a clue what she's talking about.

"You want to go for a walk or something?"

She pats the arm of the chair. "Not much of a walker, Boone. Why don't we head on back to Gram's so I can tell her about the best surprise I've ever had. She'll have fresh coffee, she always does around now, and it's far enough along in the day that she'll probably lace it with a little brandy."

Sylvia has coffee and some cookies with raisins and walnuts, and, like Molly said, she puts a little brandy in the coffee. Frankie is starting to make herself at home here, and Bert and Ray are getting used to having her around. I get why Molly says she can't imagine a better place to live. Makes me wish I had something like this.

When Molly tells Sylvia about the ramp, she looks over at me and I swear she looks like she's about to cry. She doesn't, though, and all she says is, "How very nice of you, Boone."

This all feels really good, and that makes me think that I'm about due to have something really shitty happen to me.

Chapter Twelve

Turns out it happens to Hannah.

Mark calls me and says, "I heard from Claire today, Boone. She doesn't want to talk to you, so I agreed to pass this along. Hannah's not living with them any more, I'm not sure what happened to bring things to a head, but I can tell you that your sister's in foster care now. She was placed with a couple who already have three foster kids.

"I have a phone number for them. They live in Middle Tennessee somewhere, and I've already spoken to them and told them to expect your call. They probably aren't going to allow you to come see her, at least that's the impression I got. I think you ought to give her a call, Boone. I think she needs some contact with you. She's lost everybody else, and this thing with Claire, I'm guessing she thinks that means she'll never see her mother again. Whatever you think of your aunt Claire, I hope you'll reach out to Hannah."

He finally stops long enough to take a breath and I say, "Let me have the number and I'll give her a call right now."

He gives it to me and says, "Good. I'm glad you are willing to do this, Boone."

"It's not Hannah I have a problem with, Mark, it's Claire. You saw how she was in your office that day, asking me to do stuff that was impossible, and that voicemail she left me was mean as hell."

"I'm going to get off the phone so you can call her, but before I do, how are things with you? The last time we talked you were pretty angry."

I start to tell him about Molly and my new job but I decide not to. Last time I told him what was going on it ended up all being about Hannah, and that's how this one is starting already. I'll tell him that stuff some other time.

"I'm fine, Mark. Things are good."

Then he asks, "Have you heard from Nancy?"

All that does is put me right back to where I was right after I hung up on her. "Yeah, she called me, and then lied right to my face. Her and Tiny both. I told you there was something going on there and you said, no, Boone, nothing's going on.

Well, either she was lying to me, or Tiny was, or they both were, and I'm done with all that. Don't ask me about either one of them again!" I'm shouting now and stop for a second to try to calm myself down.

"Listen, Mark, maybe I'll give you a call after I talk to Hannah. I got to go."

"Okay, Boone. Please call me. I'd like to know how it went, and if you need to talk about it, or, you know, anything, come by and see me."

"Yeah. Okay. I got to go."

I hang up feeling really bad about that phone call. I've always been able to talk to Mark and this time I was just shouting at him.

The woman who answers the phone says her name is Mrs. Cooperton, and when I ask to speak to Hannah she says that Hannah's only been there for three days and is still very upset.

"You'll need to keep it short, no more than a few minutes," she says, "and if this call upsets her more than she is already I'll have to ask you not to call back until she's settled."

That's it. I don't even know this woman, I've only been on the phone with her about half a minute, and she's giving me shit already. "Listen," I say. "Hannah's my sister, and I've got the right to talk to her. You need to put her on the phone right now so I can do that."

"Don't take that tone with me, young man." She sounds just like Aunt Claire. "I believe it would be better if you called back in, say, a week, and we can try this again. I'll tell Hannah you called." And she hangs up.

When I throw the phone it bounces off the couch cushion and slides underneath the tool chest, which I guess is good. I would have probably picked it up and thrown it again and maybe hit a wall or a window or something. I'm screaming at Mrs. Cooperton, and at Nancy, and Tiny, and Momma for starting all this in the first place by running off with Jake the car thief, and Frankie noses the door open and heads for the woods. It's a good thing she does, because as mad as I am, she might accidentally get hit if I throw something else. I'd never forgive myself if I hurt Frankie.

I start to leave, just get in the truck and drive, but I don't know where I'd go. My chest is heaving and I probably look like some kind of crazy man, and I don't know what to do right now to get my shit back together.

I know I need to, though. That time when I first knew that Momma wasn't coming back and I started wrecking that old dump we used to live in, I did a lot of damage. It was just a bunch of cheap stuff and back then I didn't really care. That old place was so full of bad memories that I didn't think twice about tearing it up. Everywhere I looked, I was looking at a place where something bad had happened. If I'd thought I could've gotten away with it I'd have burnt it to the ground.

Here it's different. I found this place, I'm the one paying the rent, it's my home even though I don't own it. Hell, I'll probably never own a house. This is as close as I'll get.

Damn, I wish Gamaliel was still around.

I make myself an S&S, even though I know he would have a fit to see me pour Thunderstorm into a perfectly good glass of shine. He didn't even like water in his. I take the glass outside and sit on the tailgate of the truck and try to figure out what the old man would say to me if we were sitting in that room in the back of his house.

Frankie comes back into the yard, but she stops about ten feet away from me. "It's okay, girl, I'm not throwing stuff anymore," I say, and after a second she trots over and sits up close to me. I give her head a scratch and think about Gamaliel. It doesn't take all that long to figure out that he'd tell me to stop feeling sorry for myself and get on with doing something. He'd tell me it didn't matter much what it was, but I needed to do something besides stare at my shoes and whine about how bad I had it. I can just about hear him saying, "If you don't get off your ass I'm going to come over there and kick it all the way down the hall and out into the front yard."

Thinking about him reminds me of that day I spent cleaning up his shed and getting his tools ready for him to use again, which he never got the chance to. I go into the house and open the bottom drawer of the tool chest.

It takes a couple of hours and a trip to buy steel wool and cleaning supplies, but by the end of the day I have about half of them cleaned up and I'm not nearly as mad as I was.

"Guess the old man was right," I tell Frankie.

I'm looking at the tools spread out on the kitchen counter. They remind me of the ones at Sylvia's house, and that reminds me of the list she and Molly showed me. I give her a call and tell her I'll be there tomorrow to get started.

"Wonderful," she says. "And you'll stay for supper, of course. Molly's been saying we need to have you over sometime when you're not outside working the whole time. I've been told my pork chops are edible, and we would love to have you."

I tell her that sounds great.

The next day I get close to half the list done. It's a long list of really small jobs, and none of them are anything like as bad as the rosebushes. I tell Sylvia I need to run home and get cleaned up before supper, and Molly says, "I'll go with you. I want to take a look at those books you salvaged from that other job."

On the way over I think about telling her about Hannah, but I decide to wait until I can actually talk to her, whenever that is. I'm sure not going to tell her about Nancy.

So when she says, "So what have you been up to?" I tell her about trying to reclaim the tools from the bottom drawer of the tool chest.

"I was saving the books for you."

"Good. Frankie and I will have a look while you're getting cleaned up. Unless you need some help."

I can feel my face turning red, and she starts laughing. After a second I can't help it, and I start laughing, too.

"See?" she says. "Cleans out the soul!"

"Guess you're right."

I glance over at her. She's still grinning and has one hand up on Frankie's head, scratching her behind the ear. Frankie has her eyes half closed and looks like she's in heaven.

"Afraid I haven't had the chance to level out the yard at the edge of the ramp."

"It's okay. We made it the last time."

When I get her up to the edge of the ramp she says, "I've got it from here, sweetie," and takes off toward the front door.

I follow her across, thinking about sex again. She gets to the door, opens it, and rolls over to the box. "I'll just hang out here with Frankie while you get cleaned up."

"You need anything?"

"Not unless you've got something to drink besides water."

I think about it, but just for a second.

"Well, I could mix you an S&S."

"What's that? Sounds interesting."

I tell her it's moonshine and Thunderstorm. "You know, shine and soda. S&S."

"Maybe not. That sounds like something I'd like if I was going to be here a while, but we need to get back soon. Gram likes to serve her food hot from the oven, so how about a rain check?"

"No problem. I'm going to take a quick shower and change. Let me know if you find anything in that box that looks interesting."

I grab some clothes and go into the bathroom. I think about locking the door, and then I think about leaving it open. I finally decide to close it. I take a really fast shower and get dressed before I come out of the bathroom.

Molly is right where I left her, and she's got a little stack of books beside her on the couch.

"That was quick," she says. "I'm just getting started with this."

"Anything good?"

"Don't know yet. Most of what's in this stack I've either read or have on my shelf at home, but there's quite a few more here."

We make it back to Sylvia's a few minutes before everything's ready, and Molly says, "Want to see my library?"

I say sure, and she leads me into a part of the house I haven't seen before. Her room is big, with plenty of open space, and one wall is a bookcase that goes from the floor to about three or three and a half feet up. It's full of books.

There weren't any books in our house growing up. Daddy didn't read, and I don't even want to think about what he'd have done if we had spent any money on books. I mean, there were school books around during the year, but we gave those back in the spring, and nobody in the family read. So I don't know whether this is a lot of books or not. Seems like a lot.

"That's a lot of books. You read all these?"

"Yeah. That's my favorite reading spot," she points to a corner of the room that has windows on two sides. "The light is great, except in the winter afternoons. Then it kind of glares all over the place."

The meal is really good, and Sylvia pours a glass of wine for me and doesn't ask for my ID. I tell her how great everything is, and she smiles a little. "Thank you, Boone. It's a pleasure to share a meal with a new friend."

"Gram, Boone thinks I have a lot of books," Molly says, and Sylvia rolls her eyes.

"You should have seen that place before I laid down the law. There were books everywhere. She had paths through the room, but there were piles on the floor, the top of the bookcase, everywhere."

I look over at Molly. "So that's why you're so interested in that box."

She nods. "You can never have enough books."

Sylvia shakes her head. "That girl's a vacuum cleaner when it comes to reading. I keep telling her she needs to get into a college somewhere. So where did you go to school, Boone?"

I tell her and she says, "What year did you graduate?"

Here we go.

I think about lying to them and telling them the year I would have graduated if I'd hung around, but I can't do it. This is probably going to screw things up with Molly, but it would come out sooner or later, so I decide to get it over with now.

"I, uh, I left before I graduated." I'm looking at my plate. It's mostly empty.

Nobody says anything and I'm about to tell them thanks for the meal and get on out of there when Sylvia says, "So did I, Boone, although I'm sure for a different reason than you did." She looks over at Molly. "I never told you that, dear, and since you never asked, I thought it best not to say anything. You have nothing to be ashamed of, Boone, although I don't recommend it and hope you decide to go back and finish." She clears her throat and starts to say something else, but decides not to, and instead says, "I made a cobbler for dessert. I hope you saved some room."

Molly says, "I only eat cobbler if there's a scoop of ice cream involved."

Sylvia smiles. "You think I don't know how cobbler is supposed to be served? I'll be right back with dessert." She's up and out of the room, and Molly looks over at me.

"I can't believe that about Gram."

I make myself look at her. She's not looking at me. She's looking at the door to the kitchen.

"She never told me. Not a word."

She turns to look at me, and I say, "We all have secrets."

Molly nods, backs away from the table, and says, "Excuse me for a minute."

She disappears into the kitchen and I can hear her voice, and Sylvia's, but I can't tell what they're saying.

Frankie's looking up at me from her spot under the table. I say, "I should have lied, girl, or just kept my damn mouth shut."

I don't hear anything from the kitchen now, and I'm trying to figure out what to do when Sylvia comes through the door with two bowls.

"I hope you're still hungry, Boone," she says. "I may have overloaded your bowl a little bit." She puts the bowl in front of me and sets her bowl down at her seat. Molly is nowhere to be seen, and I'm afraid to ask about her. I'm about to anyway when she comes through the door with a bowl in her lap.

"You didn't need to wait on me," she says. "I looked at my bowl and decided it didn't have nearly enough ice cream."

The cobbler is delicious, and nobody says a word about school or dropouts or anything like that.

"Sylvia, that was a great meal," I say. "We'd better get out of here, but we'll be back tomorrow to finish that list of jobs."

Sylvia nods and Molly says, "Actually, I think it's a beautiful night for a drive." She looks over at me. "Unless you have something else planned."

I look down at Frankie. "What do you say, girl?" She thumps her tail a couple of times and I say, "She'd love to. Where are we going?"

Chapter Thirteen

We start out the same as on our last drive, but Molly says, "Take the next right," and we end up on roads I've never been on before.

Turner's Landing dead ends into a little circle, and there's nothing in front of us but woods and water.

"Cherokee Lake," Molly says. "Shut off the engine, Boone."

I roll down the windows and for a few minutes we sit there not saying a word. Molly scoots over right next to me and I put my arm around her.

I keep waiting for her to say something, and finally she does. "Gram told me why she dropped out of high school, and it's going to take me a long time to sort that out, because it directly affects me. I understand it, though. From what she told me tonight she really didn't have a choice."

She stops talking then, like she's waiting for me to go ahead and tell her my story.

"So I guess you want to know about me," I say.

She shakes her head. "Not now. Sometime, yes, absolutely. Tonight I just want to relax. I've had enough surprises for a little while."

"Okay," I say.

We sit for a while, and she says, "You should see this in the spring, when the lake is full. They have to draw down the levels over the fall and winter so they'll have room to accommodate the spring rains."

She points out the window. "It's better that we're here at night. It's nice now, but during the day it's pretty ugly." She talks a little more about lakes and water levels and finally stops.

We sit there for probably fifteen minutes, not saying a word, and then she says, "It's so good to be able to be with somebody and not feel like you have to keep talking all the time. You know what I mean?"

I nod. "Sure do. Me and Gamaliel, we used to go for a good hour without ten words passing between us."

"That's an old name. Is he your grandfather?"

I shake my head. "I wish."

She doesn't say anything, and after a minute I say, "He lived up the hill from us. He, he died a couple of years ago. Gamaliel was maybe the best man I ever knew."

I end up telling her all about the old man. She knows about the moonshine already, so I don't have to leave anything out. When I tell her about him shooting me she starts laughing and then says, "I'm sorry."

"No," I say. "You're fine. We used to laugh about it ourselves once we got a little distance from it."

I don't tell her about Nancy and not much about Tiny, but even without them there's a lot to tell. When I stop for a minute she says, "I hate to say this, but I think you'd better take me home. It's late."

"Not that late, is it?" I turn on the instruments and it's almost 11:30. "Damn."

"I thought so. It's a good thing Gram likes you so much, or you'd be in deep shit."

I laugh out loud at that. "Darlin', I've been in deep shit so many times I can swim in it."

"Now that's a disgusting picture that I may never get out of my head," she says. "Let's get out of here. Tomorrow morning will be here before you know it, and I understand you have a job to go to and can't afford to be late."

"I got to tell you, Molly, I hate to let this evening go." I try to think of something fancy to say and end up kissing her instead.

It's close to midnight when we pull into Sylvia's driveway. I get Molly's chair out of the back and bring it around, Frankie hops out, and I get Molly settled in.

"Back in the truck, girl, we've got to get home," I say. Molly waits until I get Frankie back in and says, "I had a great time tonight, Boone. Let's do it again real soon."

"Definitely," I say. I walk with her up to the door and give her a goodnight kiss. I open the door for her and she rolls through, spins around, and says, "How about one more?"

On my way home I tell Frankie, "I've never been around anybody my own age that was as easy to talk to as Molly is. She's great."

I guess it used to feel that easy around Tiny, but not now. Not any more.

It feels like I'm leaving a lot of stuff behind. I mean, I still want to hang on to Mark, even though he really pisses me off sometimes, but there's nothing else back there for me now. The thing is, I don't feel bad about it at all. That place has all kinds of bad memories and damn few good ones.

"What I need to do now," I tell Frankie, "is not fuck this up. Nobody up here has to know that I'm nothing but white trash unless I tell them. Or act like trash. They'll know then."

The next week while I'm out getting groceries I run by the Wal-Mart and get a calendar and a notebook. I have two more jobs, both of them from Sylvia's friends, and I want to make sure I don't forget to show up. If this is going to work I have to keep people satisfied with what I do for them.

The notebook is so I can write down what I want to say to Mrs. Cooperton when I call back. The last time I blew it, and I know I did. It was too soon after hanging up from that call from Mark when he asked me about Nancy and I unloaded on him.

I make a little list:

I know you are trying to take care of Hannah.

She means a lot to me, and I just want to stay in touch with her.

Last time we talked I was rude, and I'm sorry.

That last one's going to be tough to say, since she sounds so much like Aunt Claire.

I don't know what else to write down, so I stop there and dial the Cooperton's number.

"Hello."

"Hi, Mrs. Cooperton. This is Boone Hammond, Hannah's brother. I'd like to say hi, and talk to her for a minute, if that's okay."

I hate this. I feel like I'm sucking up to this woman I've never even met. I keep looking at my list of things to say.

"Well, Boone, I'll check and see if she's done with her homework. Can you hold on just a minute?"

What the hell just happened? Why is she being so nice? I had all this stuff written down to say, and I'm not going to need any of it.

She comes back to the phone. "Hannah will be here in a second. She's starting to get settled in, so please don't say anything to upset her."

"Yes, ma'am, I understand. I just want to make sure she's okay."

"I can assure you she's in good hands. I hope you're not going to give her some kind of bad news about her parents, are you?"

"Ma'am, I haven't heard from Momma or Daddy in a long time. If she asks about them, that's all I can tell her."

She's quiet for a minute, and then says, "I'm sorry about your family circumstance, Boone. It must be difficult for you, too, even though you're older. Hannah's in a good home now, and she's . . . well, here she is. Not too long, now."

"Boone? Is that you?"

"Hey, kid. How are you?"

She starts sniffling. "I thought I wasn't never going to hear from you again."

"It's okay, Hannah. I'm doing good. I've got a place to live, and Frankie, remember my dog Frankie?, she's doing good, too. She's real good company for me."

"I liked Frankie."

"She's a great dog. Tell me how you're doing. Are they treating you right?"

She tells me she's got her own room, and there's some other kids living there, and the Coopertons are real nice. She tells me they do home schooling and they're real religious.

"They make us go to church twice a week and we have to pray before we eat anything, but Aunt Claire was already making me do that, so I'm kind of used to it."

"You sound good. You sure you're okay staying with them?"

She does sound okay. I didn't realize how much I was worried about that until right now.

"Yeah, I'm fine. When are you coming to see me?"

"I'm going to ask Mrs. Cooperton about that the next time I call. She told me to keep this short, so I'd better let you go. I'll call again real soon."

She starts sniffling again, and I say, "If they think I'm making you upset they won't let me call you again. Try not to cry, now."

She sniffs a couple more times and then says, "Okay. Okay. I'll stop."

"Listen, you be good, okay? If Mrs. Cooperton is still there, let me talk to her a second."

"She's right here. I'll see you," and she sounds like she's about to cry again. The next voice I hear is Mrs. Cooperton.

"Ma'am, I just wanted to say thanks for taking care of my little sister. She sounds good, and I'd like to call her once a week or so if that's all right with you."

I feel like I'm about to cry myself, but I'll be damned if I'm going to while I'm talking to this woman.

"That's very nice of you to say, Boone, and we'll take very good care of her. I believe it will be good for Hannah to hear from you on a regular basis, so by all means call back in a week or two."

"Thanks, ma'am. You have a good day now."

"Goodbye, Boone."

After I hang up I do start crying and it's a good two or three minutes before I can stop.

Frankie noses up under my hands and when I look up she goes over and stands beside her bowl. I go from crying to laughing just that fast.

"All right, Frankie, I know, it's time to eat."

I fill her bowl and look in the refrigerator. There's not much there.

"Looks like I might be going out for food," I say. "I wonder if Molly wants to grab a bite. Maybe bring it back here."

When I call Sylvia says, "She's in the shower right now, but I'll tell her to give you a call when she gets out."

"That'd be great, Sylvia, thanks. I was going to ask her if she'd be interested in getting something to eat."

"I can tell you right now she would love to, but she can't, not tonight. We're having some family over for supper and there are some things we need to discuss. It's rather personal, or I'd ask you to join us."

"I get that, Sylvia. Tell Molly I'll call her in a day or two and we can do something then."

"She'd like that. Molly really likes you, Boone. That's obvious to anyone who sees you together."

"She's really great, Sylvia. But you know that already, right?"

She laughs. "I do indeed. Talk to you soon."

After she hangs up I turn to Frankie. "I'm going to drive through somewhere and get some food. You want to come along? I won't be gone but just a minute."

Frankie's already at the door, so I guess she's riding along.

There's a barbecue place I've driven by a dozen times, and they have a drive-thru. I get the pulled pork plate with slaw and baked beans, and a fudge cake for dessert.

It's no Interstate BBQ, but it's not bad. I think about Razz, and wonder if he's still working at the Interstate, or if he got fired for taking off in the middle of his shift.

I wonder what P. J. would think of my working with C&R. I'm thinking she would approve, since Randy was so opposed to killing the animals he trapped. That Mississippi boat ride with her and Joaquin was the best thing about Memphis.

I'm real glad Melvin pushed me into that trip. The ocean I could take or leave, but Raymond and Charlotte were great, and New Orleans started out awful, but I ended up with the Armstrongs, had some really good gumbo, and the night I spent with Billie was amazing.

I guess the phone call with Hannah has got me thinking about stuff, and there's one thing that's pretty damn clear. Almost all of my best memories are from some place besides where I grew up, and I'll bet when Hannah gets a little older the same thing will be true for her. I think it's better that we're both out of that place, and aside from visiting Mark, I can't think of a single good reason to go back.

Chapter Fourteen

I'm getting in the habit of marking off the day on the calendar just before I go to bed. I don't want to not show up for a job, or show up on the wrong day. The little jobs I've been doing give me enough for rent and electric, so I'm doing all right for money. I'd like to keep it that way.

Molly's stack of books is still sitting next to the box from the guy's shed, and I sit down and start looking through them. I never did much reading growing up, just what I had to, but she sure seems to like it. I bet she has a hundred books in her room.

Damn. Some of these things are like five hundred pages long. There's no way I could make it through one of them. Looks like all of them are two or three hundred pages, so I'm not seeing anything here that I'm likely to read.

There's one that has a picture of a cabin in the woods on the cover. *Walden*, by some guy named Thoreau. I like the cover, so I sit down and read the first little bit. I think he's trying to say that living out on your own and not worrying too much about making money or owning a bunch of stuff is good, and I agree with him, but he sure takes a long time and uses a lot of words to get around to saying that. I put the book back on the stack that Molly has made of ones she's already read. Maybe I'll ask her about it sometime, see if it's worth wading through all Thoreau's fancy writing to get to what he's trying to say.

I go back to working on the tool chest and the tools I can get back in shape, and I've been at it for about an hour when the phone rings. It's the guy with the shed that I cleaned out, where I got the box of books and the tool chest. He sounds really worried.

"Boone, when you cleared out that shed, what did you do with the tool chest? I know I told you I didn't want any of that stuff, but turns out I need that chest. I'm hoping you didn't take it to the dump."

"Well, you know, you did tell me to get rid of all that stuff, so I didn't think it mattered what I did."

It's a really nice chest, I've spent a bunch of time cleaning it up, and there's all those tools. I know exactly what Daddy would have said right now.

And that tells me exactly what not to say.

"But I thought I might be able to use it, so it's sitting here in my living room. I've been trying to get those old tools in some kind of shape. They were awful rusted."

He's not talking to me, but I hear him say, "He kept it. He's got it." Then he's back on the phone. "Any chance you could bring that back over here sometime today or tomorrow?"

"Sure, I can do that. Let me put everything back in there and I'll load it up."

"You can keep the tools, Boone. I just need that chest back."

After I hang up I look at the chest. It's just a regular old chest, nothing fancy. I was pretty sure I'd gone through it when I first brought it home.

There's nothing in the first drawer, or in the second. The last of the skinny drawers has a rubber mat that I was going to pull out after I dumped all the old screws into the trash.

When I lift the mat up and see the envelope under it I figure that's what he needs back. I think about calling him and asking if he just wants me to bring the envelope over, but when I think about it, I don't really need this big old thing. It takes up so much space in the living room I have to walk around it, and I can get something smaller to keep the tools in. I might as well take the chest back to him.

After I get it unloaded at his shed, which is starting to look pretty good with all the remodeling he's doing, he goes straight to the third drawer and lifts up the mat. When he sees that the envelope is still there he takes a real deep breath and turns to me.

"Thanks, Boone, and thanks for not throwing this away. When I told my brother I had cleaned out the shed he freaked out. It scared the hell out of him when he thought it was gone. Turns out he had put this envelope in the drawer for safekeeping years ago and never told me. It's family records, letters, some more old stuff that wouldn't mean anything to anybody else, and I have no idea why he left it there instead of taking it to the bank and putting it in our box.

"Anyway, thanks again, Boone. Some of this stuff there we have copies of, somewhere, but not everything, and, like I said, it's no good to anybody else. Means a lot to us, though."

It's hard for me to understand why he's so grateful. I don't have any family records and if I did I'm pretty sure I wouldn't be interested in keeping any of them, but it's pretty clear he's glad to get this back. He's probably got better memories than I do. "I'm just glad I didn't take it to the dump. And thanks for the tools. I think some of them I can get into good enough shape to use sometime."

"You're more than welcome. This old thing looks a lot better since you cleaned it up. Maybe I'll hang on to it."

He offers to give me some money and I tell him to forget it, that I'm just bringing back something that was his to begin with.

I drive back home thinking about Mark, and that picture on his wall, and about just doing the right thing when the chance comes along without worrying about anything else.

Maybe I'll give him a call in the next day or so.

The next time I see Molly is a couple of days later when I pick her up to go out to eat. Actually I guess we're eating in, since we're heading for that barbecue place to get something to go.

Back at my house the first thing she says is, "It looks better without that big tool chest in here. I could barely get around it."

"Yeah, the guy wanted it back, and it was too big for me to keep, so I took it to him the other day."

"So I heard."

She's next to that big box, sorting through the ones she didn't get to the last time, and I'm sitting on the end of the couch sipping on a beer from the six pack Molly had picked up on the way back. She looks over at me and grins. "Word gets around, Boone. Gram and I heard about the missing family stuff before you did. Brandon called Gram all worked up, couldn't even remember which number in his phone's memory was yours, and got your number from her. Called us back after you left and told us all about what a fine young man you are."

I can't help but smile at that and she says, "Don't let it go to your head, sweetie. You'll start thinking you're too good to hang around with the likes of me and Gram."

I try to put on a serious face and say, "I promise I won't let it —" and that's as far as I get before I start laughing. She's smiling at me and I'm thinking this is about as good as it gets.

"So, when do you want to eat?"

I shrug. "I can eat anytime, but if you're in the middle of something there we can wait."

She shakes her head. "I'm good to stop anytime. Let's eat before it gets cold."

While we eat I tell her about Razz and his boy Diablo, and P. J. and Joaquin and the boat ride, and the acrobats on Beale Street.

"Okay, next trip you have to take me with you," she says.

"Definitely," I say. I shake a rib bone at her. "This is okay, but I can tell you Memphis does barbecue better than these guys ever thought about."

She nods. "I've heard about Memphis barbecue. Of course, Texas says they do it best, and so does South Carolina."

"I don't know about all that," I say. "Melvin just told me about Memphis."

"Can I see his map?"

I go out to the truck and get the map. After I clear all the stuff off the table I open it up. She leans forward and I realize the table's too high for her to get a good look. "Sorry. I don't have a coffee table or anything. How about if we close that box back up and lay it on that?"

She shrugs. "I'm used to this kind of stuff. No big deal."

Seems like a big deal to me. I'm watching her at the map and thinking there's all kinds of stuff I don't even worry about that's a hassle for her. It's probably better if I don't talk about it, so instead I start telling her about the route I took, tracing it while I talk.

She gives me a look when I tell her about Jericho and her crew. "I never thought of you as a prejudiced person."

That makes me think about Billie. "I'm not, it just, you know, caught me by surprise, is all."

"Okay," she says. "So where next?"

The way she says "okay" makes me think she doesn't believe me. That pisses me off a little, but I keep going.

She thinks I'm some kind of hero when I tell her about getting rid of those guys hassling Raymond. "I think they were scared of Frankie more than me," I say.

"Frankie!" She looks over at her curled up on the couch. "You're a heroine!"

When I get to the part about the two pickpockets in New Orleans she turns back to Frankie again. "Girl, you should have told him about those two. They must have been really good to fool you, right?"

I'm trying to decide whether to tell her about Billie or not when her phone rings.

"Hey, Gram, what's up?"

She's real quiet, and her lower lip starts to tremble a little bit.

"Oh, Gram, I am so sorry. Of course I'm coming right home. We're leaving now."

She hangs up and turns to me. "Gram's best friend since high school, the one who stood by her when, well, when things happened, had a heart attack about an hour ago. She didn't make it. I'm so sorry, sweetie, but I have to go. It's family."

I'm already on my feet. "Come on, let's get you home."

She doesn't say a word all the way to her house.

I get her to the front door and she looks up at me. "I can't ask you to come in, Boone. Call me tomorrow, okay? I'll let you know how things are."

I nod. "I get it. Go take care of Sylvia. I'll call you."

She disappears into the house and I go back to the truck. I feel bad for Sylvia, but I'm feeling a little sorry for myself, too. First the thing with the tool chest and all the records, and now this.

"It's family." I never had that and, except for Hannah, I never will. It makes me want to go home and call Hannah, and if it wasn't so late I would have done it.

I get home, make an S&S, and sit down on the couch next to Frankie. "We need a family, girl," I say.

Frankie looks up at me like, "What the hell do you think we are?"

Chapter Fifteen

I wait until after lunch the next day to call Molly.

"Hey, Molly. How's Sylvia doing?"

Her voice is just barely there. I've never heard her sound like this.

"She's okay. I mean, Gram's getting on in years, so she knows this is going to be happening. When she called yesterday it was just after she'd heard. That's why she sounded so bad, I guess."

She stops talking and there's a long silence.

"Want me to come over?"

"I wouldn't be very good company, sweetie, and Gram's not here to make coffee or anything. It's just me and Bert and Ray."

I'm no good at this stuff. I don't know whether she wants to be by herself or wants company. Mark would know. Hell, Mark would just go over there and stay as long as it felt right to hang around.

"Listen, Molly, I'm not doing anything right now. I'll be over in a few minutes. You need me to bring anything?"

She says no, and then there's another silence.

"Okay, see you in a few minutes," I say.

"Okay." She hangs up and I turn to Frankie.

"I'm going over to Molly's. Want to come along?" I scratch her behind one ear. "Molly's pretty sad right now. It might be kind of quiet, okay?"

She's looking at me like she understands every word, and she probably does. We get in the truck and go over, walk up to the front door, and Molly opens it.

"Thanks for coming over, Boone. Like I said, it's just me and the dogs, but come on in if you want."

We follow her down to the kitchen and I sit at the table. Frankie curls up next to Molly's chair.

After a few minutes I say, "You want a glass of water or something?"

She looks over at me. "I'm sorry, I should be asking you that."

I wave my hand. "It's okay. I can get some for both of us, and if you want to talk . . . ." This is the kind of thing Mark does all the time. He knows how to just be there in the room with somebody if they're hurting. He did it for me lots of times, and I never realized how hard it was.

How hard it is.

After a minute she says, "Water would be good, if you don't mind. The glasses are over there," she points to the cabinets above the sink, "and there's a pitcher of water in the fridge."

I get a couple of glasses and bring them to the table. "If I knew how to use Sylvia's coffeemaker I'd make us a pot."

She gives me a look and I say, "But this is fine."

After another minute she takes a drink, sets it down, and shakes her head. "You know why this is harder on me than it is on her?"

I nod. "Yeah. I do."

She looks straight at me. "Do you, Boone?"

I shrug. "Sure. You don't want to lose Sylvia. I felt the same way about Gamaliel, and he wasn't even blood related to me."

She starts crying then, not a sound, but big tears rolling down her cheeks.

I just sit there. I hate to see her like this, but I don't know what to do to fix it.

After a few minutes she stops crying, mostly, and says, "Yeah. Selfish, right?"

I shake my head. "No. I don't see it like that."

"I"m just glad to get this out of my system before Gram gets back here," she says. "I'd ask you to take me out to eat, get me out of here for a little while, but I don't want to leave her alone right now."

"Don't worry about that," I say. "Like you said at my house yesterday, it's family."

We end up staying for about an hour and a half, not really saying anything much. Frankie doesn't move from next to Molly's chair, and once in a while she reaches down and gives Frankie a rub.

A car pulls in and I get up to make sure it can get past the truck. It's already next to the back door, so I guess I left enough room. Sylvia and a woman I've never seen before come into the kitchen and Molly says, "Ruth! I haven't seen you in almost a year. I'm so glad you could come and be with Gram."

Ruth comes over and gives Molly a big hug. She looks at Frankie and then at me. "I don't think we've met." She doesn't sound friendly.

Molly frowns. "This is Boone, Ruth, and his dog Frankie. They're friends of mine and offered to come over to sit with me for a while." I can tell she doesn't like the way Ruth is looking at me and

Frankie, like we're breaking some kind of rule by being here.

"Well, Syl and I are here now, and we can sit with you for as long as you want," Ruth is looking at me like she'd throw us out if it was her house. I look over at Sylvia but she's not paying any mind to what's going on.

I walk over to her and say, "Molly told me what happened. I'm awful sorry, Sylvia." She smiles, but it's not much of a smile.

"Thank you, Boone, and thank you for keeping Molly company. Will you be staying for supper?"

"I can't, but thanks for asking." I kind of feel like I'm in the way right now, and if Ruth keeps on looking down her nose at me I'm pretty sure I'll say something I shouldn't. "Frankie and I better get out of your way. I'll call tomorrow and check on you and Molly."

"I'll see you to the door," Molly says.

She rolls out the door ahead of me and after I close it she says, "Don't mind Ruth, Boone. She doesn't like anybody, as far as I know. She barely puts up with me. I felt like telling her off just now, but Gram and her, they've been friends for a very long time. Gram needs her right now, you know?" She looks up at me. "You know?" she says again.

"I know." I put my hand on her shoulder. "It's okay, Molly. I've been treated that way a bunch of times." I squat down to eye level. "It's no big deal." I give her a quick kiss and stand back up.

"You better get back in there. I'll give you a call tomorrow unless you call me first."

She grins. "I might just do that."

By the time two or three days have gone by she and Sylvia are both sounding more like normal. I'm not sure whether to ask Sylvia about her friend or not, but the next time I'm there for a meal she starts talking about Eleanor. The two of them were friends for over fifty years, which I have a hard time even imagining, and Sylvia says that Eleanor got her through more than one hard time.

"I bet you did the same for her, right?" Molly is in the sunroom with us. We're all having hot tea instead of coffee, and I'm starting to like the taste even though I've never really drunk anything but coffee hot.

"Well, I suppose so, but Eleanor was special," Sylvia takes a sip and sets down her cup. "Oolong was her favorite tea. That's what we're drinking now, and the way she brewed it, it was powerful stuff. I don't let mine steep quite as long."

"So this is, like, in honor of her?" I look into my cup. Sylvia had said I should put honey in it if I wasn't used to the taste, but I had my first cup straight. It's pretty strong. "She liked it stronger than this?"

Sylvia laughs. "Oh, yes. Eleanor liked a good jolt of caffeine in the afternoon. I don't like that much, and neither does Molly."

She talks some more about her friend, but none of the stories sound like any big secret, and I'm wondering what it was that happened to Sylvia that kept her from finishing school.

I look around the sunroom while I'm listening to Sylvia and thinking what a great room this is. I haven't been in this part of the house before. It's got a view of the backyard and it's big enough that Sylvia has a Christmas tree in the corner.

We never really had Christmas when I was growing up, and so I don't usually think about it much. What little money we had Daddy wouldn't let us spend on stuff like presents and decorations and I just never got into the habit of the whole Christmas thing. I realize while I'm sitting here that I need to get Molly something and when she's out of the room for a minute I move over closer to Sylvia. "We never did much for Christmas at our house, and I'm not sure how all this works, but I want to get Molly something. I don't have any idea what to get her, though. You reckon you could help me out with some ideas?"

She looks at me for a long minute and says, "I am so sorry, Boone, it never occurred to me that a family wouldn't celebrate. Of course I'll be glad to help out, although anything you got for Molly she'd be over the moon about, I can tell you that."

"Thanks, I really appreciate the help. You got any ideas before she gets back in here, or do you need some time to think about it?"

"I'll make a list and get it to you before you go," she winks at me, "and you can let me know what you get so I won't duplicate it."

"What are you two talking about?" Molly is in the doorway, and I go back over to my chair.

"Nothing."

She laughs. "You're a terrible liar, Boone."

I grin at her. "I know. I always get caught." I look out the window. "Sun's out, and it's not too cold. You up for a drive?"

"Sure. I'll go get a sweater."

She leaves again and Sylvia says, "I'll get that list ready and give it to you when you bring her back."

"I appreciate it. Maybe you better say what stores have the stuff you're putting on the list."

She lays her hand on my arm. "Oh, my. You really didn't have Christmas at all, did you?"

Now I'm starting to get a little mad, because I can tell she's feeling sorry for me. I don't like folks feeling sorry for me, and I don't want to be mad at Sylvia, so I stand up and say, "Hey, Frankie. Wake up, girl, we're going for a drive."

Sylvia says, "I'll ask you to come in for a glass of hot chocolate when you get back. Your list will be ready then."

Turner's Landing is a lot prettier at night this time of year. When I say that Molly says, "Told you so. Wait til you see it in the spring, sweetie. It is nothing like this."

She leans against me and we're quiet for a few minutes.

"Gram seems to be okay," she says.

I nod.

"So what were you two talking about when I was out of the room?"

"Nothing, really. Just talking, you know."

She jabs me in the gut. "Like I said, you are a terrible liar. Were you talking about me? Is that it? Were you asking her all kinds of personal stuff about me? You don't have to sneak around, you know. Just ask me, I'll tell you."

"I really can't tell you what we were talking about. It's kind of a secret."

She smiles. "Well, at this time of year, that can only mean one thing. Okay, no more questions. I like surprises."

After a second she says, "So, are you going back home for Christmas?"

"I am home."

"I mean, to see family, you know, like that."

This is not what I want to be talking about, but I figure I might as well get it out there.

"Momma and Daddy are both gone, my sister is in a foster home somewhere in Middle Tennessee, and I told you about my brother, you know, that Frankie's named after. So I really don't have any family to go to, and that means this is where I'm spending Christmas."

"Oh." She reaches out for one of my hands and after a minute looks up at me and says, "You can come to our house for Christmas, if you want."

I'll be damned if I don't feel like I'm about to cry. I clear my throat and say, "Don't you think you ought to ask Sylvia about that? I mean, she might have plans already."

"Oh, she'll be fine with me inviting you. She just loves you, Boone. We both do." Then she looks away real quick and says, "Frankie is invited too, of course. Bert and Ray will be put out about sharing Christmas with another dog, but they'll get over it, I'm sure."

"Well," I say, "if you're sure it wouldn't be too much of a bother."

"I'm sure. We have eggnog on Christmas Eve, and if you've never had Gram's eggnog you're in for a treat. We usually spend Christmas morning just sitting around in our pajamas, sipping coffee and opening gifts. Gram makes a really good egg and sausage casserole, and there's music, and the lights are so pretty. It'll be great!"

I realize I need to get something for Sylvia, too, so I ask Molly about that.

"Oh, Gram started saying years ago that she had more than enough stuff and didn't want any other things that she'd just have to find a place for. What she wants is to have family around, and this will be her first Christmas without Eleanor. I think it'll be great having you there, and please don't feel like you need to get us anything."

"We'll see," I say. I look over at her and she's got a little smile on her face.

"Well, I'm not going to get you anything," she says, "I mean, besides what I've already got for you."

"So it's like that," I say, grinning.

She nods. "It's exactly like that."

I wonder if this is what Christmas feels like for other people. I never understood why everybody at school and in the stores was so damn happy this time of year. It was never that way at our house, just more fights or everybody staying out of each other's way. Like any other day.

I'd really like to just relax and enjoy this, but I keep thinking I'm bound to do something to screw things up. I always do. What I'd like to do, what I need to do, is get back down to see Mark. He'd understand why I'm so afraid I'm going to mess up a really good thing.

"What's on your mind, sweetie?" Molly's looking at me with a kind of frown on her face. "You okay?"

"I'm fine," I say. "There's this guy, Mark, he's a real good friend of mine, and I was thinking I need to go see him. It's been quite a while."

"He's that preacher you told me about, when you were telling me all about Gamaliel," she says. "We've got a really good preacher at our church, I can introduce you to her and she'd be glad to talk to you if you need it."

I shake my head. "It's hard as hell for me to talk to anybody about stuff, you know, and me and Mark have already been through a lot together. Besides, I need to tell him about you."

A woman preacher. I know Daddy would probably give me a beating if he knew I was good friends with a black preacher. No telling what he'd say about a woman. Probably just laugh at me.

Molly smiles. "Well, Gram's already told Reverend Carol all about you, so that seems only fair."

Chapter Sixteen

The list from Sylvia has half a dozen things on it. Three of them are books, and I know how to buy a book. Some of this other stuff I wouldn't even know how to start.

I get one of the books and that doesn't seem like enough, so I get all three of them. A lot of the books in her room are paperbacks, so that's what I get. One of them, a book of poems, I can only get in hardcover.

The girl at the counter asks me if I want a gift bag and I guess she can tell by the look on my face I'm not used to doing this. She says, "Are these for Christmas?"

When I say yes she says, "Come over here."

There's a rack with all kinds of fancy paper bags. I hold up what I'm buying and say, "Should I put these two in one bag and the hard cover in one by itself?" I'm thinking that three books in one bag would be too much, and I'd like to have two gifts for Molly.

She nods. "The poetry in a bag by itself, for sure."

We go back to the register and she says, "You'll need a card for each bag." I think she's trying to take care of me.

"Whatever you think. I appreciate you taking care of me like this."

She smiles. "Hey, it's Christmas. These for a girlfriend?"

My face gets really red. I can feel it. She laughs and says, "Ooh, this looks serious!"

I start to tell her it's none of her damn business whether it's serious or not, but I end up laughing along with her.

"Maybe," I say.

"That's too bad," she says. "Guess I missed my chance, huh?"

For a second I don't know what the hell she's talking about, and then I realize she's teasing me.

"I better get going," I say. "I've got a couple more stops to make."

Just like that she's back to being serious. "Okay, let's total this up and see what we've got."

"She wasn't teasing you, Boone, she was flirting with you." Mark leans back in his chair and grins.

It's taken me a couple of days to get down here, and I start by telling him about Molly and Sylvia and how I'm trying to figure out Christmas, since we really never did that at our house.

"I have to say I think it's wonderful that you stumbled into this family," he says. "Every family does their celebrations in their own way, but it sounds like you're in a good place to learn."

"She's great, Mark, really great," I say. "I don't even really notice the wheelchair sometimes."

He leans forward across the desk. "For me, Boone, that's the most important thing about this. Do you realize you were probably three minutes into telling me about this great girl you met before you mentioned the chair? That says a lot about you, Boone, and about how you're maturing."

I have to look down at the floor. I'm not used to people talking about me like this. "I don't know about all that," I mumble.

"I do." He clears his throat. "You know you have to remember it's a big part of her self image, though. I think it's great that you don't notice it sometimes, but you can never forget it's there. I can promise you she doesn't forget."

I nod. "I know that, Mark."

"I believe you do, Boone. Now, how is everything else with you? You've spent," he looks at the clock on his desk, "twenty minutes here and all you've talked about is Molly."

"Okay," I say. "What do you want to hear about first?"

"Well, I am curious about Hannah, so let's start there."

I tell Mark about really screwing up the first call. "It was right after I hung up with you and I was still mad about Nancy and, well, I should've waited a day or two. Mrs. Cooperton ended up telling me to try again in a week."

Mark isn't saying a word.

"Okay, so, anyway, I wrote down some stuff to say and called back eight or ten days later, and she was as nice as she could be. Didn't even need my notes. Hannah's okay, sounds like she's in a good place, and maybe I'll go visit her after she's been there a while. At least I got the idea it'd be all right after the first of the year."

I look up and Mark is smiling at me. "Nice recovery, Boone."

I shrug. "I was stupid the first phone call. Didn't want to be stupid twice."

He nods. "So what else?"

"I guess that's it. I'm done with Tiny and Nancy, Hannah's in a place that sounds a lot better than Aunt Claire's, and Molly is, like, the best thing that's happened to me in a long while."

Mark says, "I understand the anger you must feel toward Nancy, and Tiny certainly should have been more open with you about what happened, or is happening, between them. I hope you can find your way to forgiveness, and, more than that, a way to reconcile with Tiny. He's a good friend, Boone, and those are rare."

I just look at him.

He grins a little. "Too preachy?"

I nod.

"Okay, no more about any of that. So what did you get Molly for Christmas? You told me books, but not what kind."

I get Sylvia's note out and look at it again. "I got the three books Sylvia told me about because I couldn't decide, so here," I hand him the list. "You heard of these?"

He looks at it, shakes his head, and hands it back to me.

"My advice? Hang on to this girl as tight as you can. She's a treasure."

"You can tell that from a list of three books?"

He nods. "Well, not only that. You've told me a bit about her already, and going by this wish list, she clearly has excellent taste in literature. As well as in male companionship," and he winks at me.

I offer to treat Mark to lunch, but he says he's got too much going on to take off in the middle of the day.

"I'm very glad to see you, Boone, and to see that you're doing so well. You, too, Frankie," he gives her a scratch. "Stay in touch, and a very Merry Christmas to you and yours."

"Same to you, Mark," I say, and we head back home. There's a little part of me that thinks about calling Tiny while I'm down here, but that doesn't last long, and pretty soon we're back at the house.

"I should have asked Mark about what I'm supposed to wear to Sylvia's on Christmas," I tell Frankie. "I've got a long sleeved shirt and some jeans that I don't usually work in that I can wear for Christmas Eve, and I guess I'll ask Molly about what to wear the next day."

She said that they just sit around in their pajamas and take it easy on Christmas Day, but I don't own any pajamas, so that's out. I'm starting to realize that there's a lot of stuff I don't know about, well, everything.

It's funny, I never cared about any of this until I met Nancy. I remember I had to buy some clothes just to go over to her house for dinner. Same kind of thing happened on my trip, but I sort of got by with what I took with me, which was pretty much everything I have. I'm not in any better shape now, except I've got some more work clothes, and that's not helping me any for spending Christmas at Sylvia's.

This is one time Gamaliel couldn't help me. He didn't care about any of that stuff.

Chapter Seventeen

"I think Frankie likes her present," I tell Molly.

She looks over at her and smiles. "I think you're right. Anyway, it looks good on her."

We're at the table in the sunroom, sipping coffee and finishing off the sausage and egg thing that Sylvia made. Frankie is sitting up real straight next to the tree, showing off her new collar.

"I guess I didn't realize how old and ratty looking her other one was until now."

Sylvia laughs. "You should have seen us online, looking at collars. There are hundreds, maybe thousands, of choices. I agree with Molly. It looks good."

"This is real nice," I tell Sylvia. "My best Christmas ever." I don't tell her it's the only time I can remember celebrating Christmas.

"We're so glad you could join us," she says. "I would say especially Molly. Right, dear?"

I look at Molly expecting her to be all red faced, but she's just smiling. "It is truly a fine Christmas morning, Gram."

There's paper and boxes all over the place. Bert and Ray are in their new beds, there's a fresh pot of coffee just finishing up, Sylvia has some music on so low I can barely hear it, and she's looking better than I've seen her since before Eleanor died. She's got a little smile on her face and she keeps looking at me and then at Molly and nodding.

"So what is that thing you got?" I ask Molly.

"It's an iPad," she says, "and this case that Gram picked out is so perfect."

I used computers at the school library back when I still went to school, but we never had one at home, and I've never seen one like this before.

"See?" she rolls over to me and holds it up. "I've got my first background picture installed already."

It's a picture of me buckling Frankie's new collar on.

"Well," I say. "Good looking dog. Don't know about the guy, though."

"I do," she says. "And look at this. It's got a Kindle already installed, so anytime I want a new book to read I can just download it and jump right in."

I'm thinking about the books I got her and I'm about to say something, but she's still talking.

"You know, there are some books I can go through in no time, just a good quick read. Then there are some that I want to sit and hold in my hand, and read slowly, and really treasure what the author is doing with language or whatever."

She holds up the book of poetry I got her. "Like Jane Hirschfield. I love to sit with her poems for a while, until I start getting the stuff I missed on the first read. And the way she arranges the words on the page is amazing all by itself.

"Or Cormac McCarthy. This book," she holds up *Suttree*, "I'll need a dictionary handy. His command of language is remarkable. Plus it's set in Knoxville, so I know some of the places."

She grins at me. "Like I told you already, you can never have enough books. I love these, Boone. I wonder who helped you pick them out," and she looks over at Sylvia.

"Hey," I say, "I was glad to have the help."

Sylvia gives a little wave of her hand and gets up. "More coffee, anyone?" There's a little tremble in her voice.

The rest of the morning passes slow and easy, and I can't think of anywhere I'd rather be. Molly and Sylvia aren't in any hurry to clean up the room, or get out of their pajamas, or do anything to mess with what's going on right now.

I'm starting to realize just how much of the time I spent all tensed up, waiting for Daddy to blow up about something or other. Even though it's been a few years now it's still in me, I can tell. Everything depended on that, on what was going on with him, and we never really knew until he came after one of us. I don't miss that, and I don't miss him.

I just want to keep this morning going as long as I can.

Eventually Molly says, "I'm going to get dressed and see if I can talk Boone into taking me for a Christmas Day drive. You're welcome to come along, Gram, but you'd have to sit in the back."

Sylvia laughs and says, "I believe I'll pass on that opportunity. You kids have fun, and remember to be back here in time for supper."

Molly heads for her room and I say, "You need some help cleaning this up, Sylvia?"

She shakes her head. "I'm fine. Thanks for the offer, but I think you have a job already. These rides are so good for her. She enjoys spending time with you, and it gets her out of the house. I don't drive much anymore, you know, so this is just wonderful."

I step over to her and give her a hug. It feels really awkward, and I'm not sure why I do it. It's been a long time since I hugged anybody, not counting Nancy or Molly. Or Billie. The last time I hugged Momma was probably four years ago or maybe longer, and Daddy, well, Daddy never hugged anybody and I can't imagine hugging him.

So it starts out feeling kind of strange, and I think it takes her by surprise, too, but in just a second she's hugging me right back. I'd forgotten how good it feels.

When I ease up she does too, and I step back. She's got tears in her eyes, but all she says is, "Merry Christmas, Boone."

"Same to you, Sylvia," I say, and about that time Molly comes into the room.

"I saw that," she says. "Where's my Christmas hug?"

"Sorry," I say. "Used it all up on Sylvia."

She shakes a finger at me and tries to look mad, but starts laughing. I'm already grinning, and Sylvia starts laughing right along with Molly.

"Laughter cleans out the soul," she says, and Molly says, "Definitely. Ready for that ride, sweetie?"

We've been on the road for about fifteen minutes when she says, "So, what do you think of Christmas at Gram's so far?"

I try to think of something really smart to say, come up empty, and end up saying, "It's the best Christmas ever for me. Really, the only time in my life I've ever had any kind of, you know, fun or anything."

"Oh, Boone," she says, and when I look over at her she's crying.

I can feel myself getting mad at her, thinking she's just feeling sorry for me and how I don't need that from her or anybody else. She puts her hand on mine where it's gripping the steering wheel and says, "What's wrong, sweetie?"

"I don't like people feeling sorry for me, is all," I say, and think, okay, I just took a really nice day and screwed it up.

"You're mistaken," she says. "I'm crying because I'm so happy, not because I feel sorry for you. I know what it's like to have people's pity. I would never do that to you. It's so great the way you treat me, like I'm a regular person, and when you said it was the best Christmas ever, I just started crying. It's not pity, Boone. It's not." She still has her hand on mine, and I try to relax it.

"Girl, I love you," I say.

"It's mutual," she says.

I can't believe I didn't screw things up. Usually when I feel like people are looking down on me I say whatever pops into my head, and everything goes to hell. Mark told me once I should count to ten before I open my mouth when I'm feeling that way, and I remember thinking that was some kind of bullshit thing that preachers say. He might have been right, though.

Neither one of us says anything for the next ten miles or so. I'm not going anywhere in particular and a couple of times I let Frankie choose which way we go at a T intersection. The first time Molly gives me a funny look, and I tell her about the first part of my trip, on the way to the ocean, where I let Frankie choose about half the time.

"I had to take over when we got close to Charlotte," I say. "I wasn't used to driving in cities and I wanted to make it to the ocean."

Molly nods, and then says, "Okay by me, but just remember, Gram has a fine meal in the oven and it'll be ready in," she looks at the dashboard, "about an hour and a half. Just don't get us so far from home that we're late."

We meander around for another half hour or so and then start looking for a landmark that'll get us headed in the right direction. We run back into 11W and turn south.

On the way back I keep thinking about what Molly said, about knowing what it's like to have people feel sorry for you. I'd like to know more about her, about how she ended up in a chair and what it's like having to use it all the time, but this is not the time to ask. I don't know much about a whole lot of stuff, but I do know that. I came real close to turning the best day I've had in, probably, my whole life into just one more bad day. I'm sure as hell not going to take any more chances.

If I can remember to keep my damn mouth shut.

I'll get her over to the house, mix her an S&S, and we can sit and talk about whatever. Maybe we can do that tomorrow or the next day. It's been a real long time since I've done that. Too long.

"What's on your mind, sweetie?"

Molly's looking at me and I can't tell whether she's worried or not. I swear, she is the prettiest thing.

"Nothing much," I say. "Thinking about getting you over to the house sometime soon, maybe spend the afternoon just talking about, you know, whatever."

"I'd like that," she says. "A lot."

When we get back it's still a little while before time to eat, and I tell them I'm going to call Hannah and wish her a Merry Christmas.

"You can use the sunroom if you want," Sylvia says. "I've still got a little to do before it's time to eat and Molly can give me a hand."

The phone rings half a dozen times and I'm about to hang up when Mrs. Cooperton answers.

"Hello, Mrs. Cooperton. It's Boone, Hannah's brother. I thought I'd call and wish her a Merry Christmas if she's not busy right now."

"Just a second, I'll get her."

"Hey, Boone." Hannah sounds really good.

"Merry Christmas," I say. "How are you doing?"

"It's so good, here, Boone, I wish you could be here with me. They have a tree, and presents, and we all sit around and sing carols, and it's just great."

I tell her about my Christmas and then we're both quiet for a minute. I guess we're thinking the same thing, about what it was like at home and how much better it is where we are now. It's too bad we can't be in the same place, and I tell her so.

"I was thinking that, too," she says. "So are you coming to see me pretty soon?"

"Pretty soon," I say. "I'll call Mrs. Cooperton in a few days and figure out when I can come."

We talk for a few more minutes and she tells me about the new clothes she got, and some kind of bracelet she says is just beautiful.

When I tell her what I got she says, "A jacket for cold weather I can see, but a book? You don't read, Boone!"

"Well, maybe I'm about to start," I say.

I start to say something else and she says, "I got to go, Boone, we're going to eat in just a few minutes. There is so much food here, you wouldn't believe it."

That's how I feel when I see the food that Sylvia has spread out. Molly sees the expression on my face and laughs. "You should have seen it before I got her to back off. You could have fed a football team and had half a dozen desserts left over."

So Hannah and I both get the best Christmas meal we've ever had. I end up staying at Sylvia's until almost midnight, and Sylvia finally says, "I can't stay awake any longer. As much fun as this has been, I'm calling it a night. So glad you could join us, Boone."

"Thanks, Sylvia. It was great. I'm going to take off myself here in a few minutes. See you soon."

It takes a little more than a few minutes, but pretty soon I'm on the way back home. "Well, girl," I say, "that was the best day I have ever had by a long shot."

I can't stop smiling, even after I get home and fall into bed.

Chapter Eighteen

The third week in January we get one of those warm spells and the temperature is close to 65, almost tee shirt weather. Molly calls me up and says, "We need to get out somewhere and take advantage of this before it turns back into winter."

"Sure," I say. "You got something in mind?"

There's a park not too far away that has a paved trail, and Molly wants to go there, just to get out of the house for a while. I head over, pick her up, and the three of us are at the park a half hour later.

Frankie's on one side of Molly, and I'm on the other. I've got her leash looped over one of the handles of the chair, but she's staying right next to the wheel. Molly reaches over every now and then and gives her a scratch. The trail isn't level, but it's pretty close, and that makes for easy going.

The trail is about three quarters of a mile long, and there's one spot where it comes real close to the basketball courts. One of them is empty, but there are games going on in the other two. Three guys are leaning against the chain link fence watching one of the games, and when we go by for the second time one of them says, loud enough for us to hear even though we're past them, "I always wondered what it'd be like to get it on with a cripple," and they all start laughing.

I stop and stand there for a second, trying to do that counting to ten thing that Mark told me about. It's not working too well.

"Let it go, sweetie," Molly says. She reaches to put on the brake and lays her hand on my arm. I look down at it.

"That won't stop me," I say.

She nods her head, and we head back toward the three guys, who stop laughing when we start back towards them.

It's been a while since I've been this mad. It's that old white hot anger, and I'm thinking that I might just have to take all three of them on at the same time. I can hear Mark saying, "Don't say anything, Boone, just walk away," and Gamaliel saying, "Don't waste your time on those pricks." I know that's what I ought to do, but I just don't have it in me to leave it alone. I stop when I'm on the other side of the chain link from them and turn to face them.

Frankie is all tensed up, and I can hear her growling. I don't think they can hear it. Not yet.

What I can barely hear, like he's almost gone, is Daddy. When I notice that, that Mark's voice and Gamaliel's voice are louder than his, it cools me down enough to start thinking, and all of a sudden I know what to do. I look at the three of them. They're standing, fists tight, ready to jump me if I come around the fence. I smile at them.

"I heard what you said," I say, "and from what I can see standing in front of me, it's better than anything you'll ever get."

From beside me I hear Molly say, "Damn right."

She reaches over and squeezes my hand, and Frankie nudges me with her nose. I turn and start walking on Molly's right side, and Frankie goes back to her spot beside the left wheel.

Her shoulders are shaking before we're ten feet away, and by the time we go around the curve and are out of sight she's laughing out loud.

"Oh, my God, sweetie, that was perfect!"

She twists around in the chair. "I was scared to death you were going back there to pick a fight."

"I was."

She turns away, and then swivels the chair around to face me.

"Why didn't you, then?"

I don't know how to talk about what Gamaliel and Mark did for me without talking about Daddy and how he pretty much completely screwed me up.

"It's a long story, darlin'," I squat down beside her and push the hair back from her face. "I'll tell you about it sometime."

"I'd like that," she says, "but only if you want to, and only when we've got time to go all the way through it."

I nod.

"Speaking of going all the way," she says, and now she's grinning, "you don't actually know what it's like to get it on with somebody like me, do you?"

"I've never known anybody like you," I say, and then I think, what a lame thing to say.

"I sure hope not," she says. "Anyway, one of these days, we might just have to do something about that lack of knowledge." Then she laughs.

"Those three jerks had no idea you didn't know what you were talking about."

When we get back to Sylvia's Molly can't wait to tell her about our face off with the three guys at the basketball court.

"We've never actually done it, you know," she says, "but they didn't know that. You should have seen their faces, Gram! Boone was awesome!"

I can't look at Sylvia. I mean, Molly's talking about us doing it like it's kind of a normal thing, and I think that's great, but she's talking to her grandmother. That feels really weird.

I'm still staring at the floor when Molly stops talking for a second, and when I look up she's on her way out of the room. "I'll be right back," she says over her shoulder.

"Boone?"

I look up and Sylvia's looking right at me, and it looks like she's trying not to laugh.

"You look like you'd like to crawl under that rug, Boone. It's okay, really it is. I know Molly's a grown woman, and while I might make different decisions for her if I had the power to do that, she is very much her own person. Or perhaps you haven't noticed that yet?"

I nod. "I've noticed, Sylvia. Definitely."

Her face turns serious. "But I will say this, or rather ask this. She means the world to me, and I don't think I could bear it if she was hurt. You seem like a young man with high moral standards, so I'm asking you to honor those and please don't hurt her."

I have to bite my tongue to keep from laughing. Nobody has ever said I had high moral standards before, and Sylvia wouldn't either if she knew half the stuff I've done.

"I have to tell you, Sylvia," I finally say, "she's starting to mean the world to me, too."

"I can tell. That's why I'm not going to worry any more than I absolutely have to."

Molly comes rolling back in. "Are you two talking about me behind my back?"

I give her a wink. "Every chance we get. Right, Sylvia?"

She smiles. "Indeed. Well, I didn't know if you two would be hungry when you got back, so I just thawed out some of that tomato basil soup I made up last summer and set out sandwich fixings. I can have the soup hot in just a few minutes, so tell me when you want something to eat."

"Gram gets a couple of boxes of Grainger County tomatoes every year and spends most of a week in the kitchen," Molly says. "We've got sauce, and soup, and tomato jam, and it's all incredible. I'm not ready quite yet, sweetie. Do you mind waiting for a little bit?"

We sit and sip coffee and I tell them about the next jobs I've got coming up.

"Nothing real big, a lot like the stuff I did before Christmas," I tell them. "Nothing as hard as your roses, Sylvia."

"I know about one of those jobs," she says. "I told a friend about your work for us, and she asked for your number. She's the one with the guest house that needs to be cleared out."

I nod. "She's coming up next week. I had a look at it two days ago, and I think I can get it done in three days."

We talk for a while longer and Sylvia goes into the kitchen to get the soup ready.

"I just can't get over those three jerks at the park," Molly says. "You handled that beautifully."

"Three years ago I would have gone after them," I say. "I had kind of a hair trigger back then."

"In that case, I'm glad you've matured. This," she pounds the arm of the chair, "makes a good battering ram, but I might have a little trouble breaking up a three on one fight." She laughs at the expression on my face, me trying to imagine her as a battering ram.

I shake my head. "You're the best thing that's happened to me in a long time."

Molly sits there for a second, her eyes getting a little teary. "Same here, Boone. Same here."

Sylvia thinks I have high morals. I sure as hell wasn't raised that way, but all that's what I'm trying to leave behind. That whole way of doing stuff the way Daddy taught me. It didn't work worth a damn for him, and Mark seems to think I've got some good in me somewhere. I hope that's not just preacher talk.

I'm starting to get why he likes that picture his brother gave him so much, and why he's got it in his office where he can look at it anytime he needs to. All those people, just paying attention and doing the right thing when the chance came around. Nothing big, nothing fancy. I bet it's a good reminder for him, and I kind of wish I had one. I got a feeling it's going to be kind of hard to hang onto this doing the right thing stuff.

Chapter Nineteen

I don't understand how people can throw away
some of the stuff they do. The guest house I'm
supposed to clean out is all the way at the back of
the yard, and the lady that hired me says she's
been using it for storing stuff for a long time and
she wants it all gone.

"I'm moving to South Carolina, where the rest
of my family is, and I can't take all this with me,"
she says. She wants everything gone, to the bare
walls, she says.

That makes sense, I guess. I mean, moving to
be close to family and not wanting to haul a bunch
of stuff across the Smokies. But I'm barely started
when I go back up to the main house.

"Ma'am, I just want to make sure you don't
want any of this," I say when she comes to the
back door. "Some stuff back there is almost new."

She says she knows that, and doesn't want to keep any of it.

"That's my old life," she says. "If there's something back there you want, you're welcome to it."

When I get back to the guest house Frankie is on her feet, growling a little way down in her throat. She's locked in on the open door.

"Oh, hell, girl, is there something in there?" I get close enough to take a look inside. What I see is boxes and piles of all kinds of stuff and enough room to walk through the house, but nothing is moving.

"Where the hell is Randy when I need him?" I call Frankie up to the door, but she's not moving. There's only one thing I can think of that would do that to her.

"It's a snake, right?" I move one box out into the yard, then another. I'm moving the third box when I get just a glimpse of the back third of a big snake heading back under the rest of the boxes. It looks like it might be a copperhead. I know there's a corn snake that looks a lot like a copperhead, but I didn't get a good enough look to be sure. I go back up to the main house. When the woman comes to the door she looks like she's getting tired of me bothering her, but I figure she needs to know this.

"You've got a snake, at least one, in the house," I tell her. "It might be a copperhead, but I didn't get a good enough look at it to be sure. I don't have the traps or anything like that to relocate it."

She stops me right there. "Kill the damn thing!" Up to now she's been real calm and proper, but now she's all worked up and is closing the door while she says, "Let me know when it's dead!"

I shrug and go back down to the guest house. On the way I stop at the edge of her garden. Good thing she hadn't put up her tools from last season. There's a hoe leaning up against the fence and I take it down to the house.

"You get up in the truck, girl," I say. "I can't have you getting snakebit."

She really doesn't like it when I put her in the cab and close the door. I make sure I have the key in my pocket in case she hits the lock. That happened to a friend of mine once, but the car was running, and he ran out of gas before the guy with the slim jim got there to pop the door open.

"It'll be okay, Frankie," I tell her. "I'll get this snake taken care of and let you right back out, I promise."

It's a good thing I got here pretty early in the morning, because it takes me a good part of the day to clear out enough of that first room to find where the snake ran to. The only two doors to the room are behind me when I get down to that part of the room, so it's backed into a corner. There's three more boxes right in there with it, but I hook them with the hoe and drag them to where I can get my hand on them and push them out of the way.

I hate the idea of killing an animal, but I figure this is kind of like that rabid raccoon I shot back at Gamaliel's old place, the one that was facing off with Frankie. This one's a copperhead, for sure, and it's a good thing there's still power down to this house and I can turn the lights on. For what seems like a long time we're just there in the room together, both of us waiting for the other one to make a move.

It looks like it's willing to just wait me out, so I take a step toward it. It's watching me, and I know an animal without any way to escape is the most dangerous kind. I'm into it now, though, and I can't call Randy or anybody else. If I leave, the snake will take off or move to another room and I'll have this all to do over again.

"Okay, snake, let's get this over with," I say. I take another step.

I can't tell whether it's watching me or the blade of the hoe, but when I move the blade it follows it, barely moving its head. One more step.

The snake is getting ready to do something, I can feel it. It's going to take at least one more step to get close enough to swing the hoe, so I take a deep breath and step forward.

I wish to hell that lady had taken better care of her tools. That old hoe is so dull, it takes three or four swings to make sure the snake's dead. I back out of the room and go out to the truck, sit down on the front bumper, and try to get my breathing back under control.

Frankie is going crazy in the cab, so I get her leash, let her out, and clip it on her new collar. She's straining hard to get into the house, like she knows the snake's dead, and I have to really lean back to keep her from charging on in there.

"Girl, I just wanted to let you see I'm okay. I got to get rid of that thing before I let you in there just in case." I take her back around to the back of the truck and lower the tailgate. We're sitting there, I'm drinking a Thunderstorm, and Frankie's having some water when the woman, her name is

Mrs. Linwood, opens her back door and says, "Did you get it?"

I nod. "I got it, just need to take a second and I'll go back and pick it up, get it out of there."

"Thank you so much," she says. "I can see why Sylvia recommended you. Stop by and see me before you leave for the day."

Her property backs up to a pasture and I hook the snake with the hoe and carry it back to the fence. I toss it over, under some bushes that are growing up close, and go back to the guest house. There's enough stuff in the yard from me trying to find the snake to give me a full load, so I pick all that up and pile it in the bed. By that time it's close to quitting time and I won't be able to make another run, so I get Frankie in the cab and drive back up to the main house.

"Mrs. Linwood?" I knock on the door and in just a second it opens.

"Are you okay, Boone? I was worried out of my mind about you going after that awful snake."

I shrug. "It was no big deal. I'll come back tomorrow and try to get caught up. I know I told you three days to finish, but that's thrown me a little behind. I only got the one load that's in the truck right now, and that's it for today."

She gives me a little smile. "Oh, I think you've done enough for one day, Boone. And I won't hold you to that three day estimate. Take as long as you need."

When we get back to our house I turn Frankie loose and go straight to the kitchen. I pour a little shine into a glass, start to add Thunderstorm, and say, "The hell with that," and drink it straight down. The next one I make with less shine and a couple of ice cubes, and fill the glass with Thunderstorm. I take it out to the truck and sit on the tailgate, sipping.

After a while I start going through the stuff I took out of the house. Most of it is definitely junk and I pile it off to the side. There's one small box of books I set aside for Molly to look at, and a pair of work boots that are a little too big for me, but I figure with an extra pair of socks they'll be just fine.

The only other thing in this first load I decide to keep is a CD player/radio that works fine when I plug it in.

The rest of the job is easy, just takes an extra day. Some of the stuff in the kitchen is hard to throw away, but I don't really need it. There's a rack in the bedroom closet that probably has fifty or sixty ties on it, all kinds of weird colors and patterns. There's all kinds of clothes, too, and I can't make myself just throw them away, so I call Sylvia and tell her what I've got.

"There's a thrift store in town that would love to have all that stuff," she says. "Don't take it to the dump, Boone. Take it to your house and we'll figure out what to do with it in the next day or two."

That evening she calls me and tells me she's checked with the thrift store and they'll take any clothes I bring them.

"They won't pay you anything for them, you understand," she says.

"I'm not looking to sell them, Sylvia. I just hate to waste all these good clothes."

I remember the first time I got invited over to Nancy's house for supper I went to a thrift store and thought they had great stuff. Now I'm on the other end of all that, helping them stock the shelves.

So I got a few things for the house, found a way not to throw away all those good clothes, plus Mrs. Linwood gave me a $50 bonus for getting rid of the copperhead. My next job isn't for a couple of weeks, so I've got time to hang out with Molly.

Things are pretty good right now, and I'm thinking I'd like to go see Mark again. I usually go down there when things are really shitty, so I can surprise him this time. Maybe I'll take Molly.

Chapter Twenty

Even though the sun's shining, it's too cold to sit out in the yard, so Molly and I are in the house. We've finished the sandwiches we picked up for lunch and are just relaxing.

I take a sip of my S&S. Molly has one I made about half strength, and she's moving slow on hers. I set the glass down and say, "So, I've been meaning to ask you. Remember that time you asked me out for a beer and when you found out I wasn't twenty-one you showed me your license?" She nods. "How did you get a license? I mean, you don't have one of those cars that are set up for hand controls, right?"

"I never told you how I ended up with this fine piece of transportation, did I?" She taps the arm of the chair. "It happened when I was sixteen, about three months past my birthday."

"So you already had the license when . . . ." I don't know how to ask about this. It feels like I'm being nosy, but I really want to know. I mean, it seems like it's something important.

"When I got paralyzed?" She picks up her glass and takes another small sip. "It's okay, sweetie, it's not a secret. It was in the papers and everything."

I don't read the papers, so if it, whatever it was, was in there I wouldn't have seen it.

"There is a place in the Great Smoky Mountain National Park, the Sinks. You heard of it?"

I shake my head.

She looks at me for a second. "I thought you were from around there. Well, anyway. The Sinks is a real popular place to go wading, swimming, take pictures, hike, all that stuff. What you're not supposed to do is dive off the cliffs into the pools.

"It was stupid, but all of us were doing it. There were about eight of us altogether, and we were taking turns going into the water. My foot slipped just a little bit right as I started to jump, and I didn't make it out far enough to clear the rocks."

She stops for a second.

"They tell me I almost didn't make it. Lifestar had to come get me, and I spent a long time in the

208

hospital and later on in the the Patricia Neal Rehab Institute in Knoxville."

She stops again, longer this time.

I start to say something, but I'm not sure what to say. So I just sit there, feeling stupid.

Finally she looks up. "That's one of the things I love about you, Boone. You know how to let it be quiet without rushing right in there to say some silly thing I've heard ten thousand times already."

She laughs, but it's an angry kind of laugh.

"Bet you wish you'd never done that. Were you all drinking? God must have plans for you if you made it through that all right. Kids these days just don't think, do they?" She looks at me and she's about half mad and half sadder than I've seen anybody in a long time. "There's more, but you get the point, right? I tell you, Boone, I've heard them all, a hundred times over."

I take another sip and wait.

"Not that you would say anything like that, I know," she says. "You've got too much class."

That makes me laugh out loud.

"What?"

"Nobody's ever accused me of having too much class before," I say. I wave the glass around and the ice rattles.

"Matter of fact, it's been pretty much the opposite."

"You know, after you were so great with those three guys at the basketball court, you said you were going to tell me sometime about what made you change from a guy who picks fights to the kind of guy who can do what you did to them." She looks at me. "I've got some time right now, and you just heard my story. Let's hear yours."

I take a deep breath. "Careful what you ask for, Molly."

When I look over at her, she's sitting with her hands in her lap, looking right at me. "I'm here, sweetie. Not going anywhere."

"All right," I say. "I have to start with Daddy."

I tell her about how Daddy just went from one job to another, always getting in trouble. I tell her about how we'd know what kind of night it was going to be by the way he drove into the yard and whether he slammed the truck door or just closed it. About his hand, and how he blamed the kid that cut his sleeve to keep his whole arm from getting pulled into the baler. About what a mean drunk he was, and how we spend a lot of our time trying to stay out of his way. I tell her about my brother Frankie, and what a great guy he was, and how he could sometimes make Daddy laugh when nobody else could, and how much better Daddy liked him than me. About how he wouldn't let Momma take Frankie to the doctor when he got that cut on his arm until it was too late and the infection was so bad he didn't make it.

"After that, Momma was pretty much gone already, she just kind of sat around being sad," I say. "And Daddy, well, we thought he was mean before. Before was nothing compared to after we lost Frankie."

Frankie comes trotting over and sits real close to me. I look up and Molly's got tears in her eyes.

"You sure you want to hear this?"

She nods. "Every bit of it."

There's no way I'm telling her all of it, but I keep going, telling her as much as I can.

I tell her about Daddy and Momma both disappearing on the same weekend, and Momma calling to tell us Hannah is going to live with Aunt Claire. About meeting Gamaliel and what a great man he was, and how he taught me to make shine and all. "Some of this part you already know," I say, and she nods again.

"You tell it however you need to, Boone. Don't worry about repeating yourself."

I tell her about Jerry and the problems I had with him, and about Nancy and how at first I thought I was some kind of charity project for her and then I thought it might be real.

"She helped me through Gamaliel getting sick and dying," I say. "I'll have to give her that. Course she might have been lying to me all along and I didn't find out until a little while back."

I shake my head.

"Anyway, Gamaliel's funeral is where I met Mark, and he's turned out to be great, just great."

I tell her about working at the home, and how I saw Mark treated bad just because he's a black guy, and how he tries as hard as he can not to get too preachy around me, but sometimes he can't help himself.

"I'd say Gamaliel taught me more about how to just, you know, stand up in the world and not pay any attention to all the assholes around, but not to take any shit from them either.

"Mark, now, Mark taught me about listening to people, and figuring out what's really going on, and forgiving. I'm still working on that part."

I look around for my glass, pick it up, and drain it. "And then there's Momma. After she took off and sent for Hannah, she got hooked up with this guy Jake and as far as I know, she's still with him, somewhere. She helped him steal my truck, or I guess Daddy's truck, and he'd have done it, too, if it hadn't been such a piece of shit that it broke down on the side of the road. He didn't even make it to the next county."

I tell her about Gamaliel's money, and how he had me hide it from Jerry, and how it was in the truck when Jake stole it but he didn't find it before he took off.

"How much money are we talking about?"

I shrug. "I don't know. $20,000.00, maybe?"

She stares at me.

"You have that much money? Where is it?"

"I spent some of it on the truck," I wave at the front yard. "The rest of it's in a safety deposit box. I'm trying not to spend it. It still feels like his money, you know?"

Molly smiles. "I get that."

"I told you about my trip, up to the pickpockets in New Orleans, and that's when you got the call about Sylvia's friend Eleanor."

"Right."

So I tell her about the rest of the trip. She laughs out loud when I tell her about Miles and the hot sauce, and nods when I tell her about me telling them why I was okay being around black people.

"That's another thing Mark did for me," I say. "I never knew any black people, not really. Daddy called them niggers and hated them about as much as he hated Mexicans, but he was wrong about that. All the way wrong."

Then I tell her about Billie, and she says, "Wait a minute. Your first time was with a black woman?"

I nod.

She starts laughing and it's a good minute before she can stop. "Oh, my God, what would your daddy say?"

"After he finished beating my ass, he'd probably say the same thing Neil said."

I tell her about what Neil said at Tiny's and how I wanted to slam his face into the charcoal grill.

"But I didn't," I say. "I just insulted him and left."

She's still laughing a little, but motions for me to go on.

"Anyway, the thing with Neil was after I got back, and so after New Orleans, Memphis was the only other place I stopped."

I take a long breath and sit for a second.

"Well, I'm sure I left some stuff out, but that's kind of my story."

I actually left out quite a bit, but I figure what I said is enough to scare her off if she's going to be scared.

She's quiet for a little bit and says, "That's quite a story, sweetie."

I nod.

"I think between my story and yours, we've had enough serious talk for today."

I nod again.

"I do want to say, though," she hesitates and I think, here it comes. After everything I laid on her, I wouldn't want to have anything to do with me, either.

"I do want to say that stuff like that can make you bitter and mean, or make you stronger. I'm glad I'm getting to know you now, because I love the man you've turned into."

I don't know what to say to that.

"So, anyway," she says, "I'd like a refill, a little stronger this time, and you said something about another box of books from your latest job? Gram and I heard about the monster snake you battled with nothing but a garden hoe, by the way. Mrs.

Linwood's a talker, so I'd say half the county knows about you by now. You might have to hire a staff to handle all the work you're going to get out of this."

I take her glass. "That's too bad. I was kind of liking this work a few days, hang out with you a few days, and like that."

She motions at me. "My refill, please. All you have to do is hire me as your office manager, and I'll make sure you get plenty of time off."

Time passes slow and easy for the rest of the afternoon, and I'm thinking I could get used to this. I've heard that you never know how bad you've got it until you're out of it looking back, and I guess that's true. I wonder if it's true for how good you've got it, too.

Molly eventually calls Sylvia to find out if we need to pick something up to eat this evening, and she tells her no, she's got something already cooking.

"Just call when you're headed this way," she tells her. Molly has her phone on speaker, so I can hear her and I say, "We'll do that, Sylvia."

"Hello, Boone," she says. "You'll have to tell me about your adventure at Jean's when you get here, but her story is going to be hard to top. She tells me the snake was ten feet long and all you had was a pocketknife."

I'm grinning and Molly is too, and I tell Sylvia I'll work on making my story better before we get there.

She hangs up and I sit down next to Molly. "I sure am glad Ralph gave Sylvia my number to get that rosebush out of your yard."

"Yeah," says Molly. "It's working out, isn't it?"

Chapter Twenty-One

The next job I get is a real pain in the ass.

Partly because of the guy that hires me, and partly because of what it is he's got me doing.

It's another one of those clean out jobs. Seems like I'm getting more of them than anything else. The thing that's different about this one is, it's the guy's attic that he wants emptied out so he can turn it into a playroom for his kids or something like that.

The only way in and out is a ladder that drops down from a trap door in the ceiling of the upstairs hallway. So everything I move has to come down the ladder, across the hall, down the stairs, and out into the front yard. Like I said, a real pain in the ass.

About half of it is in boxes and I can take care of those pretty easy, but there's also all kinds of stuff up there that I don't know how in the hell they got it into the attic in the first place.

There's a metal frame that's got a plastic horse on springs, I guess for kids to ride on when they're real little. It's not heavy, but it barely fits through the trap door. He's got an old file cabinet that's so full of papers I can't hardly get the drawers open to take them out. And there's a bunch of other stuff like that, that's just awkward as hell to move.

Back in the corner there's a big canvas thing, looks like a giant sausage on a chain. When the guy sees it he says, "Damn, I wondered where that thing got to."

I wrestle it down the ladder and stop in the middle of the hallway. "What is this thing, anyway?"

"It's a heavy bag," he says, which doesn't mean a thing to me. He can tell that by the look on my face, I guess, because he says, "You know, for boxing practice. There should be a pair of gloves up there somewhere close to where you found this." He pulls his fist up so it's right in front of his heart, flexing his arm muscle.

"You wouldn't know it to look at me now, but I was pretty good. My coach thought I might be good enough to try out for the Golden Gloves, but I did a number on my knee working on the farm and had to give it up."

The only kind of fighting I ever knew anything about was the kind that didn't have any gloves or rules or anything like that, so I'm curious.

"So, Golden Gloves is what, a tournament?"

He nods. "Right. I don't know how it works now, it was a long time ago that I was in it. I'd love to keep that heavy bag around, just for the memories, but I guess it ought to go. When you find the gloves, set them aside for me. I'll hang on to them."

So the bag goes out into the yard with all the other stuff he wants hauled to the dump. The next trip up I find the gloves, all dusty and beat up, but when he sees them I swear it looks like he's about to start crying.

"God, that was fun," he says. "I miss those days." He takes the gloves out into the back yard and dusts them off.

When he comes back inside he says, "There should be a photo album up there somewhere. Don't take that to the dump, okay? Set it aside for me. It'll probably be close to where you found the bag and the gloves."

So what ends up happening is, he decides to keep about half the stuff I haul down to the front yard, and I have to put it all in a separate pile from the stuff I'm hauling away. Then, after I get everything cleared out and it's all swept clean, he has me haul the stuff he's keeping back into the attic.

I'm telling Molly about this the next time I'm at Sylvia's, and Sylvia says, "I understand that all too well, Boone. There are things here that I should get rid of, but they are like lifelines to some wonderful memories. When I'm gone, and someone comes into one of these rooms and picks up, say, that teapot," she points to the pot sitting on a shelf over the stove, "they will see it as ordinary. To me it's anything but."

When Carrie told me she wanted me to move into Gamaliel's house and take care of it until they could figure out what was going to happen, I couldn't wait to leave that old place I was living in. The only things I took out of there were some clothes, the stuff Gamaliel had me keeping for him, Daddy's shotgun, and a few things to remind me of my brother. Somewhere along the way I lost all of Frankie's stuff, and I guess if somebody found them for me I'd probably get all emotional too, like the guy with his boxing gloves. I'm sorry I lost that stuff, but all the rest of it, and there wasn't much, I didn't even think about saving.

So I got no lifelines, like Sylvia has, to help me remember things. Which in my case is good, I think, since most of my memories of growing up are bad ones, scary ones, stuff I'm trying to forget, not remember.

I don't know why that makes me so sad, but I guess it shows, because I feel Molly's hand on my arm.

"Sweetie, what's wrong?"

I start to try to pretend that everything's okay, but this thing I've got with Molly is different. I'm not worried so much about saying stuff in front of her. So I tell her, looking at the floor the whole time. After a second I look up and Molly's still got her eyes on me. I shrug.

"Most of the time I'm glad I'm leaving all that shit - sorry, Sylvia, I mean stuff - behind, it's just that sometimes, you know, I get feeling sorry for myself. It's stupid, but I just can't help it."

There is what seems like a long, long silence and finally Sylvia says, "Try not to be too hard on yourself, Boone. You and Molly are moving away from childhood and creating your lives, and it's only right that you should look forward. People like me, and the man with the boxing gloves, are trying so hard to hang onto the past partly because we have more time behind us than ahead of us. You are just the opposite. There will be plenty of experiences that, years from now, some small item will serve to bring it all back to you. The best you can hope for is that many of those experiences will be good ones.

"That teapot, for instance," and she points again to the shelf, "is nothing special until you know that Bobby and I regularly had afternoon tea with the Sunday New York Times crossword and used to compete to see who could solve the most clues. It was a lovely way to spend an hour or two, and Bobby and I had so many of them." She looks into my eyes for a long moment. "It took years to create that memory, and it's one of my best. So, you see, I could never part with that old thing, even though I don't use it any more.

"I don't know what you've been through, but if it was unpleasant there's no shame in leaving it behind. We've all got things in our past we'd just as soon forget."

Molly has been quiet through this whole thing. I look over at her and she's staring at me. She says, "Boone's told me about some of the stuff he's been through, Gram, and you're absolutely right. I think you're due a few good memories, sweetie. Actually, on that trip you just took, that afternoon on the Mississippi River might qualify as one, and definitely your night in New Orleans." She winks at me.

I'm thinking about Hannah, and her having such a good Christmas with the Coopertons, and me spending Christmas with Sylvia and Molly. I wink back at Molly and say, "Sure, but I think Christmas with you two is going to be a great memory, too."

"One of many to come, I hope," says Molly.

Sylvia looks over at her and says, "Why, Molly dear, you're blushing!"

After supper I say, "That talk about memories is making me think I'd like to go see my sister Hannah. She's in foster care and I haven't seen her since, well, for quite a while."

"That's a wonderful idea," says Sylvia.

I look over at Molly. "You want to come along? It won't be for a while yet, I've got to call and set it up, and I'll probably want to go see Mark first, get some advice about how to handle this. Anyway, think about it. I'd be glad of the company."

"I don't have to think about it," she says. "I'd love to go with you."

"Great," I say. "I guess I'd better let Hannah know you're coming along. She doesn't know I've got a, you know . . . ."

Molly laughs. "You can say the word, Boone. It's not hard."

Now I'm embarrassed, but I'm not mad. I used to get so mad when I got embarrassed.

"Okay," I'm grinning, "she doesn't know I've got a girlfriend."

"See?" She holds one hand out toward me. "You said it and nothing bad happened."

Chapter Twenty-Two

I guess word's starting to get around, like Molly said would happen after I took care of the snake in the guest house. That and the weather is starting to warm up a little bit. I'm glad I bought that calendar. For the next little while I've got a job of some kind every week. All of them are two or three days long, which is fine with me. I'm working about as much as I want to.

Most of the ones I'm getting now are outside work, clearing brush and shit like that, people getting ready for spring. The guy that Sylvia told me about, who wanted stuff to fill up the gully in one of his fields, is happy about all this work I'm getting. It means he doesn't have to deal with anything himself, and still gets his gully filled.

"The way this is going, in another month or two you'll have to find some other place to haul your stuff," he says on one of my trips. "My cousin's got a place down toward Knoxville, a big gully right through the middle of one of his best fields, but he's real particular. No trash, no garbage, all he wants is brush and dirt."

He gives me his cousin's number, so I've got two places I can use to get rid of stuff, not counting the county dump.

Most evenings when I've got work either I'm over at Sylvia's or Molly's at my place, and at least once a week we get together during the day and go out for a drive or lunch or something.

"I think I'm going to visit Mark next week," I tell her one day when we're on the way to pick up sandwiches for lunch at Sylvia's. "You want to come along and meet him? I've told him a little about you and he said he'd love to meet you."

"Are you sure?" She sounds a little nervous. "What if he doesn't like me?"

"He will. If he doesn't, I'll just kick his ass," I say. "I've threatened to do it before and never got around to it."

I call Mark to give him a heads up and also to make sure he's not got a meeting or a funeral or anything, and we figure out a day and time. "I'm looking forward to it, Boone," he says.

We get there in the middle of the morning and when we get inside, Betty is standing in the middle of the hallway not far from her office, talking to some guy in a suit. She sees me and says to the guy, "Would you wait in my office, please? I'll be right there."

She grabs me and gives me a hug that goes on for long enough to make me a little uncomfortable. Betty and I were never that close. She's all over Frankie, too, and Frankie's eating it up. Then she straightens up and turns to Molly. "Hi. I'm Betty, the administrator here. I take it you're a friend of Boone's?"

Molly sticks out her hand and Betty shakes it.

"Betty, this is Molly, my girlfriend. Molly, Betty was my boss while I was working here."

"Girlfriend? Well, well," says Betty. "It's very nice to meet you, Molly."

"You, too, Betty," says Molly, and then we all just stand there for what seems like an awful long time until Betty says, "I'd love to stay and talk, but I told Mr. Campbell to wait in my office and I really should go see him."

"It's fine, Betty, we'll just head on down to Mark's office. I called him the other day and told him we were coming."

"Boy, she was uncomfortable," Molly says when Betty's office door closes.

"Yeah, well, she was more my boss than my friend," I say. "Let's go see Mark."

"It was more than that," Molly sounds worried. "I think she disapproved of me."

I know that sometimes Betty can come across real unfriendly, which is pretty strange when you think about what her job is.

"I don't think it was you, darlin'. I've seen her act that way around people before, and it doesn't mean she doesn't like them. She's just thinking about running this place all the time, and she doesn't ease up even for a minute."

The other thing, which I don't say to Molly, is that she's good friends with Nancy's family and she might be thinking that I ought to be with her instead of somebody new.

Frankie is a few steps ahead of us and pushes Mark's door open with her nose and goes right in. I hear Mark say, "Hello, Frankie! Did you bring anybody with you this morning?"

"Sorry, man," I say when I push open the door the rest of the way. "I'm trying to teach her to knock before she goes into a room, but it's going to take a while."

Mark comes up to me and grabs my hand. "It's good to see you, my friend," he says.

I notice that one of the chairs that usually sits in front of Mark's desk is over in a corner. He turns from me to look at Molly, who has rolled up beside me.

"So this is the famous Molly," he says with a big smile. "Welcome."

"And you are the famous preacher Mark," she says, and her smile is just as big.

"Come in," he says. "Boone, would you go down to the cafeteria and bring us some coffee? You know how I take mine, and I imagine you know how Molly takes hers as well."

"I think I just got invited to leave," I say, grinning. I look down at Molly. "You want some coffee?"

She nods. She's got kind of a question on her face, but she says, "That'd be good, sweetie. I'll keep an eye on Frankie for you."

"Thanks, Boone," Mark says. "Close the door on your way out, will you?"

It takes me a few minutes to get back, and I have a tray with three cups of coffee and four or five donuts. I can hear voices on the other side of the door, but when I open it they get quiet.

"Here we go," I say, and Mark leans over and clears off a corner of his desk. I hand around the coffees and start to take a sip when Molly says, "I'd like to say a blessing, if that's okay."

I'm pretty surprised, since we never do that at Sylvia's or anywhere else, but I figure since we're in a preacher's office, why not.

Molly keeps her eyes open and on Mark when she says, "Thank you for this hot coffee and good food, and thank you especially for this fine man who has told me so much about my dear Boone and how best to care for him, and may I be forgiven if I accidentally roll over my sweetie's foot with my wheel. Amen."

I laugh and say, "He'll be preaching on that last line one of these days. Right, Mark?"

I look over at Mark but he's not looking at me. He's looking at Molly, and when I turn my head I see big tears rolling down her face. Her hand is shaking. I'm afraid she's going to spill her coffee, so I take it out of her hand and set it on the tray.

I turn back to Mark. "What the hell did you tell her, man?" Molly has hold of my hand now, and she's squeezing it so tight it's almost hurting.

Mark's voice is soft, and he's talking as much to Molly as he is to me.

"I told her the truth, Boone.

"She asked me to tell her about you, and I told her you are sometimes reckless, that you are a damaged young man who has been deeply hurt, and as such are capable of hurting others. She asked me if being with you is worth the risk, and I said absolutely. I said you have a core goodness and decency that is as strong as any I've seen, and that you are worth whatever she can invest in your relationship. I told her you are one of the finest people I know."

He breaks eye contact with Molly and looks over at me. "I hope that you came here assuming that I would tell her the truth if she asked."

I try to think of something to say and come up empty.

We sit in silence for at least a minute before anybody says anything. Finally Mark says, "Too preachy?"

I nod, grinning at him. "A little bit."

Molly says, "Can I have my coffee back now, sweetie?" I look over at her, and she's not crying any more. She has a big smile on her face, and she squeezes my hand when I pass her the cup.

We eat and drink for a few minutes without talking much, and then Mark says, "So, how are things with you, Boone? I've spent all of my time so far with this lovely young woman, and I'd also like to know how you are doing."

I tell him about the jobs I've had, and about Christmas at Sylvia's, and talking to Hannah. I tell him about the three guys at the basketball court, and about getting a book for Christmas, and the ramp at the house. I don't tell him anything about Tiny and Nancy, even though Molly already knows about that, because I figure it would just stir up old feelings.

"I'm sure I'm leaving some stuff out, but things are pretty good right now. I mean, Molly's great, but you already know that, and I'm getting plenty of work, and Hannah sounds like she's okay.

"Actually, one of the reasons I wanted to come see you is we're going to go visit Hannah in a few weeks, as soon as I get it set up, and if there's anything you think we need to know to, you know, make it go better . . . ."

Mark leans back in his chair.

"My initial thought is to make the first visit a short one. I think you should assume that there will be more visits, and not try to do and say all that you want to in this first one. Also, it's been a while since you've seen each other, and I know

234

that you have changed, matured. It would be safe to assume that Hannah has also.”

“Would it be better if I didn’t go along?” Molly is looking worried.

Mark shakes his head. “I don’t think so. Boone, you said that Hannah sounds happy, right?”

“Yeah, she sounded great.”

“Well, then, her seeing that you are also happy is probably the best thing that can happen in this first visit.”

On the way back out to the truck we see Betty again and she gives us a wave. She’s still with the suit and it looks like he’s getting the grand tour.

Once we’re loaded up and on the road, I glance over at Molly. “So, what did you think of Mark?”

“Are you kidding? It’s like Gamaliel handed you off to the exact person that you needed to meet.”

We’re coming up on a gas station, and I pull in to an empty space over on the side, shut off the engine, and sit there staring out the windshield.

I’ve never believed in any of that supernatural bullshit, mind readers, fortune tellers, any of it, but I’ll be damned if it doesn’t seem like what Molly just said is exactly what happened.

I look over at Molly. “You know, I’ve never believed in any of that kind of shit.”

She shakes her head. "Me neither, sweetie, and I'm not saying that's what happened. Just that it seems like it, that you really needed Gamaliel, and then you really needed Mark."

I nod. "Yeah, it's kind of spooky. I never thought about it like that. Not until you said it."

She laughs. "Didn't mean to freak you out. I think Mark is great, better than great maybe. He loves you a lot, you know."

I'm kind of uncomfortable thinking about a guy loving me, but I know she's right.

"Mark and me, we just understood each other almost from the first minute," I say. "Never had that happen before, even with Gamaliel. With him it took a while before he'd let me in, you know, and Mark has been right there, from the start, never had any doubt about him."

Molly lays her hand on my thigh. "What you two have, it's so strong and solid. I just hope you and me can have that kind of love someday."

I look over at her. "Might not take as long as you think, darlin'."

She shakes her head. "The stuff you two have been through together, and I'm sure I don't know the half of it, there's no quick way to get to that. I love you a lot, Boone, and we've got a really good start. What you and Mark have is different, obviously. I'm really glad you introduced us. Meeting him helped me understand a lot about you."

I start the truck and head back out onto the road. We drive without saying anything for a few miles, and I say, "It'd take quite a while to tell you about everything, but I guess you're right. We have been through a lot together. I never cared much for preachers, mostly because Daddy always said they were all a bunch of judgmental liars who were just after your money, but Mark, he's the best. The best."

"He feels the same way about you, sweetie. Listen, I know we just had those donuts, but I'm kind of hungry. Why don't you let me buy you a sandwich or something?"

"I could do that. And some onion rings."

Chapter Twenty-Three

We pull out of the Cooperton's driveway and start towards home. I look over at Molly and say, "Well, that could have gone better."

She nods.

A minute later she says, "There's no way you could have known, Boone. Nobody knew."

"I just hope this doesn't screw things up for Hannah," I say. "She really likes that place. Maybe I ought to pull over here and call Mrs. Cooperton."

Molly shakes her head. "I'd wait a while, let things calm down. Maybe when we get back to your house."

After we're back at my place and in the living room I say, "I'm going to call her. What was that other kid's name?"

"Samantha, I think. They called her Sam."

I take a deep breath. "Here goes."

The phone rings twice and Mrs. Cooperton says, "Hello, Boone."

"Hi, Mrs. Cooperton. I just wanted to call and see how Samantha was doing."

She sighs. "We're still trying to sort it all out. I can tell you her reaction to seeing your dog Frankie surprised and, to tell the truth, scared all of us. We had no idea."

"I feel awful about this, ma'am. I sure didn't mean to upset one of your kids."

"Oh, we don't blame you, Boone, or your dog. As I said, none of us expected that reaction. Sam was clearly terrified of Frankie, but your dog was still at least fifty feet away, on a leash, and wasn't threatening her in any way I could see. I actually thought when the phone rang it might be Sam's caseworker. I called her as soon as you left. I expect that there's something in Sam's history that will help us understand this. At least I hope so."

"I appreciate your not blaming us, ma'am. It sure wasn't our intention. Hannah seems to be real happy there and I just wanted to come see her and let her meet my girlfriend." I look over at Molly and she nods at me.

"Listen, Mrs. Cooperton, I'm going to get off the phone here," I say. "You're expecting that call. Tell Hannah I'll give her a call in a day or two."

"I will, Boone," she says. After a second she says, "I think at least for the time being that any visits will have to be either without your dog or in some kind of neutral setting. Sometimes we use the local library."

"I get that. I really don't have anybody to leave Frankie with, so maybe I can talk to you sometime about that library thing."

She says okay, and I hang up.

I turn to Molly. "Don't know how much of that you heard, but they don't know why she freaked out. They're waiting for Sam's caseworker to call them, maybe something happened wherever she was before."

"It must be awful, being a foster kid and getting bounced around from one place to another. I think your sister got lucky, sweetie. I know I didn't really get a chance to meet Mrs. Cooperton, but she seems like a real nice lady."

"Yeah, I think you're right. Guess I ought to call Mark, let him know about what happened since I asked his advice about how to do this." I shake my head. "He said a short visit at first."

Molly laughs. "Well, it was that."

When I tell Mark what happened he says, "I'm so very glad Mrs. Cooperton didn't blame you and Frankie for what happened. So you think Hannah isn't going to get any blowback from this?"

I don't know what blowback is exactly. "You mean, do I think she's going to take this out on Hannah? No, I didn't get that from her."

"Good, that's good. I don't know Mrs. Cooperton at all well, but she seems to be a good-hearted person. I'd be surprised if Hannah suffered because of this."

Molly says that Sylvia is planning on fixing supper for us, and since it's already the middle of the afternoon I find some pretzels in the kitchen and pour us a couple of Thunderstorms. I put a little shine in mine and Molly says, "Just a drop for me, sweetie."

I bring everything into the living room and set the bag of pretzels on the couch. When I hand her the glass I say, "I need a coffee table or something in here. Maybe I'll try to make one."

"Ugly as sin, but sturdy?" She grins.

"Yeah. Maybe that'll be kind of my style."

Molly gets real quiet after that and when I look over at her, she's staring at her glass. She says, "I know you told Mrs. Cooperton you didn't have any place to leave Frankie, and I just want to say I'm sorry you feel like that."

I had never even thought about going to see Hannah without taking Molly along, and I tell her that.

"I didn't want to promise that Sylvia could watch Frankie without asking her, and I always just sort of assumed that the next time I go to see Hannah that you'd go with me."

"Really? So it's not because I'm, you know, in this thing?" She pats the arm of the chair.

"Hell, no!" I say, loud enough to get Frankie's attention. She gets up from her corner and trots over.

"No, it's not that," I say, trying to talk a little softer. "I want you with me, darlin', not watching my dog so I can go do stuff."

"You sure?"

I nod. "Look, I'm still figuring this out, all right? I know you can't climb stairs and stuff like that, but I don't spend my time thinking about what you can't do because you have to be in that chair."

She shakes her head. "That's the thing, Boone. Most of the time I don't feel like I have to be in this chair. It's more like I get to be in it. Do you know where I'd be if I didn't have this?"

I don't know if I'm supposed to answer or not, but she doesn't give me a chance.

"I'd be in bed, or sitting in a room someplace staring at the same four walls all day long. This chair doesn't hold me back, it sets me free. If I compare myself to you, or Gram, then I'm a poor handicapped girl. But I'm not you, or her. I'm me, and when I compare myself to what I'd be without this chair, I like what I am.

"I won't spend my time thinking about all the stuff I can't do. I know people that do, including some 'non-handicapped' people, and they're just sad."

I'm trying to think of the right thing to say here, and it's really hard. I don't want to screw this up.

"Molly, you're the bravest person I know." That's how I start, and that's as far as I get before she stops me.

"No, I'm not, Boone. I'm just Molly. Just a person like everybody else. I mean, I've got this chair, but I'm not letting it define me. Like you've got your history, and you're not letting that define you either."

She stops and looks at her glass. "Didn't mean to go on like that, sweetie. How much shine did you put in here, anyway?" She looks over at me and winks.

"I'd say I got it about right." I empty my glass. "You want some more of these pretzels?"

"No, I'm good. If I eat too much I won't want any supper, and Gram will think I don't love her anymore if I turn down her cooking."

While we're eating Sylvia's pork chops we tell her about what happened at the Cooperton's.

"Oh, that poor girl," she says. "Imagine being scared of Frankie."

Frankie hears her name and comes around to Sylvia's chair. "None of this for you, dear," she laughs. "I try not to feed dogs from the table, even dogs as beautiful as you."

She refills her glass. "More ice tea, anyone?" When we say no she takes the pitcher back to the refrigerator and brings in a plate of cookies.

"For dessert, whenever you're ready," she says. "So when are you going to see Hannah? And what are you going to do with Frankie?"

"I'm going to give them a chance to figure out what's going on with Samantha, the kid that got so scared," I say. "So for now, it's going to be either phone calls or meeting at the library. Mrs. Cooperton says they do that sometimes."

"Well, if there's anything I can do to help," she says. She gives Frankie a scratch on her head and hands the cookie plate to Molly.

I keep thinking about what Molly said back at my house, about my history not defining me. It sounds a lot like something Mark would say, or Gamaliel if he ever said that kind of thing. He'd probably just say, "Stop wallowing in your own shit, boy. Nobody's holding you down there."

That's not exactly right, though. I think about all the people back where I grew up who figured they knew me because they knew my daddy. Sure seems like they were holding me down. Maybe the best thing I've done in a long time is move up here. For one thing, I met Molly, and that's turning out better than I ever thought it could.

I look over at her. She's trying to decide which cookie to take and I guess she feels me looking at her. She turns and gives me a wink. "Got your eye on any of these in particular?"

What I've got my eye on is her, and all of a sudden I'm thinking about sex. It happens to me unexpected, just out of nowhere. One of these days I got to ask her how that works with somebody like her. No, that's not right. I don't care about how it works with anybody else. Just her.

She's looking at me like she knows what I'm thinking about, so real quick I say, "I'm thinking you look good, so you better decide quick before they're all gone."

She starts laughing, and when I look at Sylvia she's got a smile on her face too, and I realize what I said and I can't help but laugh. "I mean, they look good. The cookies."

Molly says, "I know exactly what you meant."

Chapter Twenty-Four

"Let's go down to Knoxville for lunch this Saturday."

Molly is sitting on the front porch of my house reading one of the books I found in the last place I cleaned out.

"Sure, if you want to. What's down there?"

I remember the last time I went to Knoxville it was with Nancy to a music concert on Market Square. I'd never seen anything like it before, and it scared the hell out of me. Compared to Bourbon Street, though, Market Square is no big deal.

"What's down there in the spring and summer is the Farmer's Market. There's a restaurant down there that has outside tables, and we could get some lunch and just look around, you know? I never get down to Knoxville and I hear it's really nice. They have crafts and stuff for sale, too."

"What about Frankie? I mean, I could leave her here if I had to, but I'd rather not."

"They tell me the Square is really pet friendly. I think she should come along."

We get there about ten in the morning and start looking for a place to park.

"If we had a handicap sticker," Molly says, "we could park right next to the Square. We should get one for the truck."

Since we don't have one, we end up three or four levels up in one of those big garages they have close by. Finding a place to park that has enough room for me to get the chair up next to Molly's door is a real pain in the ass, but I finally find one. I put Frankie on her leash and get Molly situated in her chair, and we go to the corner where the elevator is. It takes a long time for the elevator to get up to our floor, but eventually it does, and we come out on the sidewalk heading up to the Square.

It looks a lot different in the daytime. Last time I was here, there was a band set up over to the left of where we're coming into the square and there were people jammed up against each other from one side to the other. It was loud, and crowded, and the first time I'd ever heard music like that.

Now it's full, but people are moving around pretty easy, and there are little tents set up in rows with tables full of corn, and tomatoes, and all kinds of food. There's big boxy vans with people lined up buying hot dogs and hamburgers and stuff I don't recognize. Some of the tents have wooden bowls and stuff, some of them have clothes and jewelry. It's completely different from last time.

"Let me go first, sweetie," Molly says, and me and Frankie follow her along one side of the square.

"See, if all they see is you, they just move enough to let you pass, and then there's not room for me," Molly says. "This way they know how much room to give us."

We make it down one side and across the street, and there's a little park there with a fake stream running through it and benches to sit on.

"There's all kinds of food for sale down that side street," Molly says. "Let's get something and come back here. You can grab a bench and we can eat here in the park."

After we go up and down the row of food trucks Molly decides she wants something from Good Golly Tamale. I go for a barbecue sandwich and fries, standing in line for the food while Molly and Frankie save a bench for us in the park. It's a little tricky balancing all the food, but I make it back and I got to say it all tastes delicious. The tamale is a little weird, but Molly loves it and the bite she saves for me is pretty good.

We're finishing up and about to check out the rest of the square when Frankie stands up and starts wiggling all over, wagging her tail and acting like she's about to take off. I get a good hold on her leash and look in the direction she's looking.

It's Tiny and Nancy, coming through the park from the other side. She sees us first and lets go of Tiny's hand, but it's too late to pretend anything. She pokes Tiny in the side and points to us. When he sees us it's like he can't decide whether to keep going or turn around and go back the way they came.

Frankie is barely in control, and I have to hang onto her collar to keep her from going over to them. Molly is finishing up her drink and doesn't notice at first.

When she sees that we're both looking in the same direction and how excited Frankie is, she wheels around and sees Nancy and Tiny standing there looking at us. She says, "You know those folks, sweetie?"

"Yeah," I say.

"Friends of yours?"

"Not really. That's Tiny and Nancy. I've told you about them."

"Oh." She's real quiet for a second. "So what are you going to do?"

"Me? Nothing. If they want to come over they will. I'm sure as hell not going over there."

Tiny's talking to Nancy and she's shaking her head, looking over at us every few seconds. Finally he starts walking toward us and in a second she follows him. It's like she doesn't want to come over here, but she doesn't want to look like a fool standing there by herself. So she ends up looking like a fool anyway, trying to catch up to Tiny.

I'm watching him come toward me and thinking about the last time I saw him, in the rear view mirror of the truck, standing there in his yard. I know Mark said I need to try to find some way to make things right with him, but I don't know if I can. Maybe I'm not as great a guy as Mark was telling Molly I am.

Nancy catches up to him and, when she gets up beside him, grabs hold of his hand again. I guess she figures she can't pretend there's nothing going on, so she might as well be up front about it.

"Darlin'," I say to Molly, "I don't know if I can do this. I'm sure glad you're here with me. You keep me from doing something stupid, okay?"

She grabs my hand. "I'm right here with you, Boone, and I know you are strong enough."

I'm holding on to Frankie with one hand and Molly with the other when they stop in front of us. I can see out of the corner of my eye Nancy can't stop staring at Molly, but Tiny looks down at her, nods his head, and looks me right in the eye.

"Hey, Boone."

"Tiny." I nod. I don't look at Nancy at all, just Tiny.

"I didn't expect to see you here. You living in Knoxville now?"

I know it's real important what I do right now. Frankie has figured out that things are not the same between us, and she's calmed down some. I figure she doesn't know what to do and is waiting to see what I'm going to do. This could all go straight to hell in a heartbeat.

Mark is in my head, telling me to try to make things right, and Gamaliel's in my head, saying it's not worth hanging on to old shit, that all it does is keep me angry. I can't hear Daddy at all, and that's the best thing about this whole awful situation.

It's not easy, and without Molly right here it wouldn't even be possible, but I take a breath and say, "No, we're just down checking out the Square. Well, here I am forgetting my manners. This is my girl, Molly. Molly, this is Tiny, and this is Nancy. Everybody knows Frankie already."

"Hi," Molly says, and reaches out her hand. Tiny hesitates just a second and then shakes hands with her. After she lets go of Tiny's hand she holds hers out to Nancy, but it just hangs there in the air until she drops it back in her lap.

"So, where are you living now?" Tiny sounds like he's glad to get that first few seconds out of the way, and I got to say so am I.

"Up past Morristown," I say. "I'm renting a little house up there, at least until the owners sell the property it's sitting on."

"You'll have to let me see it sometime," he says. "I've still got some stuff of yours, and I've been meaning to call you about that old rifle. I've got a guy going to take a look at it. He might want to buy it instead of fixing it up for me. You sure you don't want to keep it?"

"No, man, I gave it to you. Your call."

This is getting a little easier. I don't know why, but it's better now that it's out in the open about him and Nancy. Things with Molly are so good I'm not the least bit jealous about the two of them.

"All right. If you're sure."

I nod. "So, what are you doing here today?"

Tiny looks over at Nancy. "Nancy's got a friend that makes jewelry, and this is her first day being part of the Farmer's Market. We thought we'd come down, maybe buy something, you know."

"Oh?" says Molly. "Which one is she?"

Nancy's having more trouble with this than I am, or anybody else as far as that goes. She tries to say something and has to cough, then turns to me. "I think she's set up on the other side of the square. She's Moonglow Jewels. You should go by, maybe pick something out for your, uh, girlfriend."

It looks like that was really hard for her to say.

"What do you think, sweetie?" Molly has my hand again. "Want to stop by there before we head back?"

I nod. "Sure, we can take a look."

Nancy can't stop looking at Molly's chair, and finally Molly has had enough. "Is there something you're curious about, Nancy?"

Nancy jerks her eyes away from Molly. "No, no, sorry, didn't mean to stare."

"It's okay," Molly says. "I'm used to it. You know, one of the things I just love about Boone is, he doesn't even really see the chair. He sees me."

She looks up at me. "We should get going, don't you think? I've only seen the one side, and then we stopped for lunch. There's the other side of the market to see, and I hear the rest of downtown is really nice, too. Maybe we can, you know, wheel around for a while before we head back home."

Tiny looks a little uncomfortable, but he doesn't say anything right away. Finally he says, "We better get going, too. Come on, babe, let's see if we can find Moonglow Jewels."

He starts to leave and turns back. "Sorry, Frankie, I didn't even say hi. How are you, girl?"

Frankie lets him pet her, but she's not jumping all over him like she has in the past.

"Let me know about the rifle," I say. "I'm curious about it. And say hi to Eunuch for me."

"Will do. See ya, Boone. Nice to meet you, Molly."

"You too, Tiny," says Molly. "And you, Nancy."

Nancy doesn't say anything to any of us, just heads out a step ahead of Tiny. I watch them go.

She looks back once, sees me watching them, and speeds up, pulling Tiny along beside her. In a second they're lost in the crowd.

I look at Molly. She's watching them, too, and when they are gone she says, "Whew! That was uncomfortable. You did great, sweetie. I'm not sure what you were worried about."

"I didn't want to lose my shit in front of both my girl and my dog," I say. "I'd never hear the end of it."

"I think things between you and Tiny went about as well as they could have," she says. "And I think Nancy was a little freaked out that you had another girlfriend, and seeing me in the chair just blew her away. She didn't know what to do or say."

I nod. "Sounds about right to me. I'm glad it went okay with Tiny."

"Me, too, sweetie." She looks up at me. "So who is Eunuch?"

Chapter Twenty-Five

When I call Mark and tell him about seeing Tiny and Nancy when I was out with Molly, he doesn't say anything right away.

"So how did it go?" he finally asks.

"It was okay. I think me and Tiny are going to be all right. Nancy didn't say hardly anything, never really looked at me, and was really freaked out by Molly's chair. Frankie was pretty confused about what was going on, but she did all right. Molly was great, really great."

"That part doesn't surprise me."

We talk a few more minutes and I tell him we'll come see him again soon. "This time we'll take you out for lunch or something."

"Sounds good to me. Take care, Boone, and say hi to Molly and Frankie for me." He starts to hang up, and says, "Let me know how it goes with

Hannah, too. I really don't think that first meeting is going to ruin things for her, but I'd like to know how that other girl, Samantha, is doing."

"I'll do that, Mark."

A few days later Molly is at my house splitting a deli sandwich with me when my phone rings.

"Hey, man, it's Tiny."

"Hey, Tiny, what's going on?"

"Well, I'm up here in Morristown, got the rest of your stuff in the back of the truck, and thought I'd bring it by if you're going to be home."

"Hold on a second." I look over at Molly. "Tiny wants to come by in a little bit."

She shrugs. "Okay with me."

I give him directions, and in about a half hour he pulls into the yard. He gets out and looks around. The passenger door opens and Nancy gets out.

"Whoa," I say. "Didn't see that coming."

"It'll be fine," Molly says. "Let's go out and say hello."

When we go out on the front porch, Frankie is right beside me. Nancy sees her and says, "Hey, Frankie! Come here, girl!"

Frankie looks at her and then up at me. "Go on," I say. "Go say hello."

She trots across the yard to Nancy, who squats down and makes a big fuss over her. Tiny is walking toward us and, when he gets close enough, says, "I hope you don't mind Nancy coming along."

I shrug. "It's fine, man."

He looks around. "How in hell did you even find this place?"

I tell him about the sign that I almost missed, and how the owners had decided to sell the property but put it off once they had a renter again.

"Lucky break," he says.

I nod. "It was that. Lucky in a lot of ways," and I look down at Molly.

Nancy comes up then and says, "Frankie looks good, Boone."

"Yeah, she likes it here. Gets to be off the leash, and she's all over the field and woods."

It's so strange, how easy it used to be with Tiny and Nancy both, and how hard it is right now. I wonder if me and Tiny will ever get back to that. There's no way with Nancy, and I don't even want to try.

"Listen, you guys want to come in and sit for a while?" Molly says. "Boone's probably got something we can find for you to eat or drink, although his fridge is empty about half the time."

"I remember," says Nancy and then says. "Oh, I'm sorry."

Molly shakes her head and smiles. "It's okay, Nancy, Boone told me that you two used to be together. So, y'all want to come inside?"

"She's got better manners than I ever will," I say. "Come on in and we'll find something to share."

Tiny says, "Why don't you help me with this stuff I've got in the back of the truck, Boone?"

I figure it's the rest of the shine we had made, and it is. "I hope you kept a little bit for yourself," I say.

He nods. "I kept my share, just wanted to get your part of it to you." He looks up at the house. "Listen, man, about me and Nancy . . . ."

I hold my hand up. "It's cool, man. Don't even worry about it."

He's quiet for a minute and then says, "I heard from the guy who was supposed to look at that old rifle."

"Yeah? What did he say?"

"Typical bullshit, needs a lot of work, don't know if I could get to it anytime soon, blah, blah,

blah. Took him about ten minutes to get around to saying it's probably worth a couple grand as it is, and a lot more fully restored."

I grin. "Well, I reckon that's your birthday and Christmas present for the next couple of years, then."

He laughs that short laugh of his.

"Last chance to change your mind, man."

I shake my head. "I gave it to you, Tiny. It's yours. You keep it, sell it, fix it up, whatever."

He looks at me. "All right. You know what this means, right?"

"What?"

"I've got to figure out one hell of a Christmas present for you next year."

We carry the jugs up to the house and are about to go inside when Nancy comes out, with Molly close behind her.

"We better get going, honey," she says to Tiny.

He looks at her and then at Molly. "Everything okay?"

"It's fine," Molly says, looking at me. "Really, it is."

"Okay, then," Tiny says. "Nice place, Boone. See you sometime." He starts toward his truck, but Nancy's already halfway there. He half turns and gives me a look like, "What the hell just happened?" but gets to the driver's side just about the time she closes the door. He starts it up and backs out around the curve.

After they're gone I turn to Molly. "You okay?"

She nods. "It's just that Nancy and I don't have a whole lot to talk about, sweetie. It got kind of uncomfortable in there while you and Tiny were at the truck."

"Damn, I'm sorry. I should have stayed in there with you."

"Why? You don't think I can handle myself?"

She doesn't sound mad, just curious.

There's nothing good I can say here, but I feel like I need to say something anyway.

"No, I mean, yes, I mean, sure you can handle yourself."

I'm stumbling all over myself and digging that hole deeper and deeper, and finally I just stop talking. When I look over at her, she's trying real hard not to laugh. It's not working.

"Having a little trouble there, Boone?"

I raise my hands up to my shoulders. "I give."

"You should," she says. "You weren't getting anywhere with that. I know you want to take care of me and all that, but it wasn't that big a deal."

"I know."

"Nancy was uncomfortable, and so was I, and finally she said, 'Maybe we ought to try this some other time,' and I said, good idea."

"I think I'm going to let you run things from here on out," I say.

She nods. "Good. You're a fast learner."

"That's probably the first time anybody's ever called me that."

Actually, Billie called me that the morning after our night in New Orleans, but I'm not going to tell her any more about Billie than I already have.

"So, what did Tiny bring you?"

"Some of the shine we made together before the fire took out all our equipment. And he wanted to tell me about the rifle."

"What rifle?"

I tell her about Gamaliel saying I needed to clean out his shed and, if I found anything in there that was worth something, to keep it hid from Jerry.

"This old rifle was up on a top shelf, way back at the wall. It's old, and might not even work, and I don't have any use for it, so I gave it to Tiny a while back. He had a guy look at it, and turns out it's worth a couple thousand dollars. He tried to give it back to me, but I figure a gift's a gift."

Molly stares at me. "Mark was right about you, sweetie. You're an honorable man."

"I don't know about all that." I'm pretty uncomfortable talking about this kind of thing. Makes me think about all the times I've not been all that honorable, or even honest.

One time when I asked Mark about that, he just laughed. "Boone, pretty much everybody has times they feel that way. I hope that one day you'll start seeing yourself as worthwhile. Then it will be easier to hear it from somebody else."

I might be getting closer to that, but I'm sure not there yet.

"You want to go back to Sylvia's?"

She shakes her head. "I kind of like it right here."

I grin. "I'm glad to hear it. You want something to drink?"

"How about an S&S?"

I mix a couple and we sit in the quiet of the afternoon, sipping.

"I was thinking," she says after a little while.

She's sitting on the couch next to me. Her hand is resting on my thigh and she's got the glass in her other hand. She sets the glass on the arm of the couch and turns toward me.

"I was thinking," she says again.

"What about?"

"You. And Nancy. And Billie. And me. I'm not sure why you would want me, Boone. I mean, they can do all kinds of stuff I can't do."

I don't say anything right away. This feels like a real important talk we're about to have, and I didn't see it coming. I know Molly is smart, and funny, and really good looking, but I don't think that's what we're getting ready to talk about. It seems like it still needs to be said, though, so I start out by saying it.

She looks at me like nobody's ever done before and says, "You are the sweetest man to say those things, but you know that's not what I'm talking about here."

"I know."

This is driving me crazy. I want to pick her up and carry her into the bedroom, but I don't know if that's what she wants, and I don't know how to ask her. It doesn't feel right to do that without asking, so I'm kind of stuck.

"I figured I ought to say all that because you said you weren't sure why I would want you. I'll tell you this, Molly, you are the best thing that's ever happened to me. I'm guessing right now we're sort of talking about what you can and can't do in there." I point toward the bedroom.

She nods. "That's what I'm talking about. You need to know there's one thing I won't do. Not because I can't, but because of why Gram had to drop out of school. I'm not ready for that, sweetie."

It hits me then, and I don't know why I didn't get it as soon as Sylvia said she had a different reason for leaving school.

Molly is watching my face. "You understand? I can't take a chance on that. I'm not ready."

"Me either, darlin'. I've barely got my own shit together on a good day. The idea of being a daddy scares me to death."

"Good. That's good." She leans back and rests her head on the back of the couch. I reach over, turn her face toward me, and kiss her.

When I lean back she touches my cheek with her fingertips. "There is a lot of stuff I will do, you know."

"Is that right?"

She nods. "If you can help me through that door over there, we can try some of them out."

Chapter Twenty-Six

Molly and I are a little late getting back to Sylvia's for supper. She's in the kitchen working at the stove and has her back turned when she says, "I thought I was going to eat by myself tonight."

When she turns around, she takes one look at Molly and says, "Well, well. What have you been up to?"

I look over at Molly. She's blushing. I'm afraid to look at Sylvia.

"Nothing with any permanent consequences, Gram," Molly says.

It takes me a second to understand what Molly just said. I'm thinking that I ought to say something, too, but I'll be damned if I can figure out what it ought to be.

Sylvia sighs. "I'm going to put supper on the table. Boone, would you help me, please?"

"Sure, Sylvia," I say, thinking I'm in some kind of deep shit here. I look over at Molly for help, but she's busy scratching Frankie's ear.

"Grab that dish sitting over there. Careful, it's hot." She's got plates in her hands and is already out of the kitchen.

I look at Molly again. She shrugs and whispers, "I can't tell what she's thinking. Usually I can, but not this time. You're on your own, sweetie."

"Boone?"

"On my way." I grab a couple of potholders and pick up the dish.

Sylvia is putting the last plate down when I come in carrying the dish. "Set it on that trivet and have a seat."

I put the dish down and sit in my usual chair.

Sylvia sits down. She doesn't say anything for what seems like a real long time. Then she takes a deep breath.

"You know, I liked you right away, Boone. You seem like a fine young man," she starts out.

"I like you too, Sylvia," I say. I'm not sure if I'm supposed to say anything or not, but I figure what the hell.

She laughs, just a little. "I know. That's one of the reasons I'm struggling right now.

"I know that you also like my granddaughter. She's without a doubt the most important thing in my life now, and I have a strong need to protect her. And that's the struggle. What I don't know is, do I need to protect her from you?"

What I want to do right now is take off, crawl under the table, pretty much anything besides be in this conversation. I can't be mad at Sylvia, she's not accusing me of anything. She's not calling me names, or giving me orders, or anything like that. This feels like a conversation between two adults, and I don't have a lot of practice at that kind of thing.

When I figure out that what Sylvia is doing is telling me what she's afraid of, I figure the best thing I can do is talk about what I'm afraid of.

"Sylvia, it's not that I like Molly. I love her. She is by far the best thing that's happened to me in a long time, maybe ever. I get that you want to take care of her, protect her. I've tried a couple of times to take care of her and she's put me in my place real fast." That makes her smile. "The thing I'm most afraid of is that I'm going to do something to screw this up. I'm trying to figure out how much to take care of her and how much to just get out of her way and let her be Molly."

"Well, we do have that in common," she says. "I don't know whether to be glad you two found each other or angry because I think you might push her into something she's not ready for."

"We've already talked about that, Gram."

Molly is in the doorway. "I got tired of waiting to be called for supper and I've been sitting here, listening, just waiting for a chance to join in."

She rolls over next to me. "When I told him I wasn't ready to take the risk of becoming a parent, he said he felt the same way. It's okay, Gram, it really is. He's not pushing me or taking advantage of me. Actually, he's pretty classy for a guy I met when he came to do yard work for you."

She reaches for my hand. "Not that there's any shame in yard work.

"His old girlfriend came by his house today," she said. "She's pretty, looks like she's got money, and she can walk. Boone didn't give her a second look. When he and his friend Tiny were outside, Nancy, that's her name, was in the house with me and kept staring at me. She obviously couldn't figure out why Boone wanted me. And that got me wondering the same thing. So I asked him, after they left, and he said I was smart, and funny, and really good looking."

Her eyes are on me now. "Not a word about my so-called handicap. No pity, no I need to take care of this poor wheelchair girl, nothing like that at all.

"You have no idea how great it feels to have that, Gram. I mean, I know that's how you feel about me, at least most of the time, but Boone's pretty smart, and funny, and good looking himself, and he wants me. And I want him right back. No babies, though. Neither one of us are ready for that."

She looks back over at Sylvia. "So are we going to eat, or not? I really worked up an appetite this afternoon." She winks at me and wheels around to her place at the table.

"What in the world am I going to do with you?" Sylvia is trying not to laugh. "Yes, of course we are going to eat. Boone, there's slaw in the fridge, if you wouldn't mind bringing it in."

I'm glad to get out of the room, so I jump up and head to the kitchen. When I get back, Sylvia and Molly are talking away like it's a regular meal, so I sit down and try to join in. I'm telling them about my next job, which starts tomorrow and is my first repeat job. It's the snake lady; she wants some brush and vines cleared out of her back yard, over on the left of the guest house, because she's afraid there's more snakes in there. Molly is saying something about needing a pair of knee high leather boots to protect me from getting bitten when my phone rings.

Sylvia has this rule, which I think is a really good one, that we don't talk on the phone during a meal. So I don't answer it, don't even take it out of my pocket. It rings again and I ignore it again. When it goes off for the third time, Sylvia says, "I think you'd better see what that is, Boone. If you don't, they're just going to keep trying. You can go in the kitchen and get some privacy if you want."

I go into the kitchen and lean against the counter. In about a minute the phone rings again, and I look at the screen. It's the number for the home where I used to work.

"Hello?"

"Hello, Boone."

"Hey, Mark, what's going on?"

"Are you at home now?"

"No, I'm over at Sylvia's. We're in the middle of supper."

"I hate to bother you while you're eating, but I thought I'd better call you right away about this."

I bet something's happened to Hannah.

"What's wrong? Did something happen to Hannah? Did they kick her out because of that time I took Frankie down there and that other kid freaked out?"

"Slow down, Boone. Nothing has happened to Hannah, at least not yet. This is not one of those bad news phone calls."

"Okay," I say. I'm not used to getting any kind of phone call unless it's Molly, somebody needing some kind of work done, or something has happened. Molly's in the next room, and I know Mark's not calling to give me a job. So if it's not bad news I got no idea what he's going to say next. I don't even know what kind of question to ask besides the one I already asked about Hannah, so I'm just standing here waiting on him to say something.

"I heard from your Aunt Claire."

"I thought you said it wasn't bad news. She won't even talk to me, Mark."

"I know, Boone, and I hope someday she can get over that. She called because she heard from your mother, and she wanted to let me know I'd be hearing from her. Your mother was asking Claire about you and Hannah. I understand finding out about Hannah being in foster care made things very tense between them, which doesn't surprise me at all. Claire evidently was so mad at that point that she wouldn't give your mother your number, but she did give her mine."

Right now I never want to have anything to do with Claire again, blood or no blood. "Damn, Mark, she is such a bitch."

"I'm guessing there's quite a bit of guilt in there somewhere, Boone. She took your mother and sister in when they were desperate, which is a good thing to do, but you were left to fend for yourself. Then, for whatever reason, she couldn't keep her promise to take care of Hannah. I'm not saying that to excuse her, just to try to understand her. I imagine she'll be punishing herself for how she handled this for a long time."

Whatever. I got no sympathy for Claire right now. "You're a better man than I am, Mark."

"I doubt that, Boone. I'm just not in the middle of it. At any rate, I expect I'll get a phone call very soon from your mother. She's going to ask a lot of questions, I imagine, and is going to want your phone number."

"What do you think I ought to do here? I mean, she ran off and left me to deal with Daddy on my own, helped that shithead Jake steal my truck, and never called me or wrote me or asked Claire about me or anything."

"Boone, I think you should talk to her. For one thing, she's your mother. For another thing, she may be in a much better place now than the last time you saw her. Also, and I know this for certain, you are in a much better place. And, she's going to be in touch with Hannah, and you're just beginning to reconnect with your sister. You don't want to be left out of this, is what I think. If you want to talk face to face, I'd be glad to, and I can tell your mother to give me a day or two before she calls you."

"Definitely. Definitely. Man, I don't know what I'd do without you."

I hear his chair creak when he leans back in it. "You're a survivor, Boone. You'd find a way."

"Can I come down there tomorrow? No, wait. I've got a job I'm starting tomorrow."

"It can be tomorrow after you finish, Boone."

"That's great, thanks. The three of us will be there as soon as I can get done with day one."

He hesitates. "Are you bringing Molly along?"

I nod. "Absolutely. I need her, Mark, I need her beside me."

There's no way I'm doing this without her.

"In that case, by all means. Call when you're on the way. Let's meet at the home, and we can either use my office or grab a bite somewhere. By then I might know more about why this is happening now."

Sylvia and Molly have finished and moved into the sunroom when I get back to the table. I take another sip of my tea and go sit next to Molly.

"Everything okay, sweetie?"

I shake my head. "I don't know. Can you go with me to see Mark tomorrow after I finish work?"

She nod. "Of course I can. What's wrong with Hannah?"

"It's not Hannah."

She doesn't say anything, and neither does Sylvia. I look at them and they're both just waiting for me to tell them what this is all about.

"Sorry I missed supper, Sylvia," I say. She waves her hand.

"I knew it was something important when you didn't come right back."

I pull in a deep breath and blow it out. "Mark heard from Aunt Claire. She won't talk to me, ever since she wanted me to go chasing off to Memphis to find Momma a while back and I told her no."

I look up at them. "The truck I had then wouldn't have made it to the next county, and Memphis is a big place, but that didn't matter to her. She's been mad at me ever since."

Neither one of them says a word.

"Anyway, Mark heard from Claire because Claire heard from Momma."

That gets a reaction.

"Oh, sweetie," Molly says, and grabs my hand. Sylvia doesn't say anything, but she leans forward in her chair.

"The way I understand it, Momma's going to call Mark."

"Why isn't she going to call you?" Sylvia asks.

I look over at her. "Because when Momma found out that Claire had put Hannah in foster care the whole conversation turned really ugly. At least that's what Mark and I figure happened. Claire wouldn't give Momma my number, but did give her Mark's." I shrug. "I wouldn't have wanted to be on either end of that phone call."

"I can understand that anger," she says. "So now what?"

"Now I go see Mark tomorrow. He's a good friend and he's helped me through a lot. I trust him, you know?"

Molly says, "He's a good man, Gram. He can help Boone figure this out. I told you about how much he helped me, and I'd never met him before."

I end up staying at Sylvia's until it's almost ten. When Frankie and I get up to leave, Molly says, "Want me to come home with you?"

Sylvia raises her head from the book she's been reading and Molly says, "It's not like that, Gram, you know it's not. I just want to be with him if he needs that."

"I know, dear," Sylvia says. "I can't help the way I react, though."

"It's okay, darlin'," I say. "I'm all right. Besides, all I'm going to do is go home, fall into bed, and get up tomorrow and go to work."

I take hold of her hand. "It might be good news from Momma, you know? I'm trying not to borrow trouble here, so I'm thinking I'll just stay busy until we get to Mark's tomorrow. I'll be dodging those huge snakes all day tomorrow and won't have time to worry about it anyway." I wink at her and she smiles, but it's a worried kind of smile.

"You sure?"

I nod. "You know, I'd love to have you at my house any time. But I really am okay. I'll call you tomorrow when I'm finishing up work."

She nods. "See you to the door?"

When we get to the front door I lean down and give her a quick kiss that turns into a long one. When I straighten up I look at her and say, "Boy, it's been a day, hasn't it?"

Molly is looking at me with those beautiful eyes of hers. "It has indeed, sweetie. This afternoon was fantastic, and this evening, well, we'll have to see how this all turns out. It wasn't exactly a quiet evening at Gram's, was it?"

"No, not quiet. Sorry I had to lay that on y'all."

She shakes her head, hard. "Don't you dare be sorry about that. I love you, Boone. I want to be here when you need me."

"You always are."

I pretty much do just what I told her I would. Go home, fall into bed, and try to sleep.

Wonder what Momma's into now.

Chapter Twenty-Seven

The next day takes forever to go by, but I do get a fair amount done, and I don't have to kill any snakes this time. At least not so far. I got to say, it looks like the kind of place a snake would just love.

I swing by and get Molly on the way back home. After I jump in the shower, we head down to see Mark, and I call him to tell him we're on the road.

"Your mother called," he says. "I'll tell you all about it when you get here, but I will say she sounds good, Boone. Of course, we'd never spoken before, so it was a bit awkward at first."

I hang up and tell Molly, "This might not be as bad as I was afraid it was going to be."

She squeezes my leg, but is talking to Frankie. "Did you hear that, girl?"

Mark is leaned against his Mini Cooper when we pull into the parking lot. "It's a nice evening, and I know a place that has a patio. They'll be fine with Frankie joining us at our table. You can follow me." He starts to get in his car and turns. "If you can keep up, that is."

I shake my head. "Don't do it, man. You know this big old thing won't take curves like that little toy car you drive."

He grins. "I'll take it slow."

The place is not too far away, and looks pretty nice. Plus it looks like it's set up so Molly can get around without any trouble.

I never used to pay any attention to that kind of stuff. As long as I could get around, I was good. Take stairs two at the time, squeeze through narrow doors, turn sideways to walk between tables at a restaurant or store, never even noticed. Now I notice that stuff all the time, and it pisses me off when folks don't make it easy for Molly to go places with me. Hell, sometimes they make it impossible. I'm pretty sure they're not doing it on purpose, but it still makes me mad.

I asked Molly once how come she didn't get mad about this stuff and she said, "What makes you think I don't get mad about it?"

This place looks fine, and we grab a patio table that has plenty of room around it in case we end up talking about something personal.

Frankie settles in under the table, and the girl serving us makes a big fuss about what a beautiful dog she is.

"I know," I say. "Hear that, Frankie? She thinks you're a beautiful girl."

Frankie thumps her tail a couple of times, and the girl grins. "So, what can I get you three?"

We order, and when she's gone I say, "So, what's going on with Momma, Mark?"

"We had a really good talk," he says. "She sounded good, especially considering what you've told me about her.

"She's not with that fellow Jake you mentioned any more. He's been out of the picture for a year or so, and she's living on her own up in Illinois. A little south of Chicago, she said. She was furious about Hannah, and we sort of expected that, and she was relieved to hear that you are doing well. She wants to call you tomorrow, and I told her I'd find out what time would be good and get back to her."

I lean back in my chair. "We need to talk about this, Mark. I mean, I'm still the guy she just left behind to deal with all the shit, and she sure took her time about trying to find out if I'm okay. And she helped Jake try to steal my truck."

He nods. "It's a lot to forgive, I'll grant you that. If you don't want to talk to her I can let her know that, but I have to say I think that's a mistake."

I look down at the table. "I just don't know if I can do it, man. I mean, is she going to try to pretend that none of that stuff happened? I've got a good thing going here now, I've got work, a place to live, the best girl in the world, and I don't want to screw that up."

"Woman," says Molly. "The best woman in the world."

Mark laughs out loud. "I told you, Boone. You better hang on to her as tight as you can. She's a treasure."

I can't help but grin. "The best woman. No doubt about it.

"But I don't know what she's going to ask me to do. I'm just now crawling out from under all that crap that Daddy laid on the whole family, and I don't want to get sucked right back into it. There were lots of times that he was going off like a crazy man, and me, Hanna, and Momma, we were just shaking in our boots, trying to stay where he didn't notice us so we wouldn't be the ones to catch whatever hell he was throwing around that night. See, I'm getting all worked up just remembering it. I'm stuck here, man. I don't want her to pretend it never happened, and I don't want her to start crying and saying how sorry she is, because I don't know if I'd believe that. I don't know. I just don't know."

Mark is quiet for a couple of minutes, long enough for the waitress to bring our food out, and a dog biscuit for Frankie. "She's a beauty," she says. "Is it okay if she has this?"

I tell her sure and she holds it out to Frankie. She sniffs it a couple of times and then takes hold of the end.

"Such a great dog. Well, y'all let me know if you need anything," she says, and heads toward another table.

Mark clears his throat. "I can see you're having a real struggle with this, Boone, and I think that's about right. I'd be worried about you if you weren't struggling. I still think that you ought to talk to her. It'll be very difficult, but I think it needs to be done. She's reaching out, Boone. Don't turn away."

"I'll be there," Molly says. "Right beside you. That is, if you want me to be."

"Hell, yes, I want you there," I say. "You're the best woman in the world."

Molly laughs, and after a second, so do I.

"Excellent," says Mark. "And now, my food is getting cold, and I am starving."

It's pretty good food, almost as good as Sylvia's, and when I say so Molly says, "Wait until I tell her that, sweetie. It'll be all over the county by the next day, and she's not usually a gossip."

"So, what time tomorrow?" says Mark.

"Tell her I have to get back home from work and clean up," I say. "About 5:30 or 6:00, I guess."

"I'll tell her 6:00," says Mark.

The next day I swing by and get Molly on the way home from work, and after I take a shower, I mix a couple of S&Ss and we sit and stare at the phone.

It rings at about a minute after six.

I look at Molly and say, "Here goes." I answer on the second ring.

"Hello?"

Nothing.

"Hello?"

"Boone, is that you?"

"It's me, Momma." She starts crying right then, and damned if I don't start, too.

Molly's right up next to me on the couch, squeezing my hand. I try to think of something to say, and I should have made a list or something. I'm blank. Finally I clear my throat and say, "How are you, Momma?"

It's the stupidest thing ever, but she stops crying and starts to say something. She starts laughing instead, and it's like she can't stop. In a minute she gets her breath and says, "I'm good, son, I'm good. That man I talked to, Mark, he says you're doing good, too."

"I am, I'm doing good. Where are you?"

She tells me the name of some town I've never heard of, and then she's quiet for a long, long time.

"Boone, honey, I am so sorry for everything. I'm so sorry," and she starts crying again.

"It's okay, Momma, it's okay. I'm glad you're doing good." I feel like a damned fool. Here I am trying to make her feel better when she's the one that left me, just left me.

I can't help it, though. I just can't stand to hear her crying like that.

"Don't cry, Momma, okay? Tell me how you're doing."

"Is it true that my own sister put Hannah into foster care?"

And there we go. Enough about me, I guess.

"That's what Hannah told me, and Mark told me. Claire won't talk to me."

"I'm going to get her out, Boone, I swear. I'm going to get her back."

This was a really bad idea. I'm just getting madder and madder the more she goes on about Hannah. She hasn't asked me anything about me. Hell, I at least asked her where she's living. She hasn't even asked me that simple question.

"Where's that no-good daddy of yours?" She sounds like she'd like to hunt him down and pay him back for how he treated her.

"He's been gone since that weekend you left and took Hannah to live with Claire."

"What do you mean, gone?"

"He's gone, Momma, I haven't seen him since that weekend."

At least I'm not lying to my own mother.

"He just left you there?"

I nod, and then remember she can't see me. "Yeah."

"How did you get by? Where did you stay? Who took care of you?"

I don't say anything. I don't even know where to start telling her about the last four years.

"Boone? Are you still there?"

"I took care of myself, Momma. That's who took care of me."

She's quiet for a little bit.

"That Mark fellow that I talked to, who is he?"

"You remember Gamaliel, Momma?"

"No, I don't, honey. Who's that?"

"The old man that lived up the hill from us. Him and me got to be good friends after, you know, and when he died Mark was the one who preached his funeral."

"He's a preacher?"

"Uh-huh."

"Well, I never thought you'd be hanging out with a preacher. What is he, Pentecostal, Baptist, Presbyterian? He's not one of those Unitarians, is he?"

"I don't really know, he's just a preacher. See, Gamaliel was in an old folk's home, and Mark works there, so he works with all kinds of people. I guess he's a little of all of them."

"I don't know about that, son. I mean, you have to decide on one church."

"You'd have to ask him about that, Momma, I don't really know." This is a waste of my time. I want her to care about me, and she's spending all her time on Hannah, and Daddy, and now Mark, and I don't want to talk about any of them.

"Are you in a place by yourself, Momma?"

"Why'd you ask me that? What did Claire tell you? Did she tell you about Jake? I'm not with him any more, not for a year or so. He wasn't a good man, son, not a good man at all. I'm better off rid of him."

I don't answer, because I don't know what to say.

"I'm in a, it's like a shelter for women who got away from men who treated them bad. There's a lot of good people here, Boone, it's a good place."

"I'm glad, Momma. That sounds real good."

"Do you ever see Hannah?"

"I just saw her once after she got in the foster home, but I'm going to go back and see her again real soon. I talk to her now and again."

"Is it a good place? I'm still going to get her out, it just might take a little while. I made a bunch of mistakes, honey, and I know that, but I'm getting stronger all the time, and the people here are helping me out a lot. I'm going to make things up to Hannah, and to you, too, as soon as I get out of here and get my own place."

"That sounds real good, Momma. Real good."

I'm starting to wonder how I can get off the phone when she says, "They're ringing the bell for our evening group meeting. I got to go, son. I'll call you again real soon."

"It's real good to hear you're doing okay, Momma."

"I love you son. I got to go."

I start to tell her I love her too, but she's already hung up.

I put the phone down on the arm of the couch and sit there. Molly doesn't say anything, just holds my hand real gentle and waits for me.

"You always know the right thing to do?" I turn to her after a while.

"What do you mean, sweetie?"

"I mean, just now, you knew to wait."

She shrugs. "The best woman in the world."

That makes me laugh, and she does, too, and everything starts to be okay again.

"Damn right," I say.

"So, you want to refill my drink?"

I get up and refill both of them, sit back down, and say, "I guess it could have been a lot worse."

I look over at her and she's right there with me, listening hard. I start to take a sip and instead just set the glass down next to my foot.

"She says she's doing good, and I think that's true. I'm trying to remember what she used to sound like, back before all this happened, and she was so quiet it was like she wasn't even there. She sounds stronger than that now. So, anyway." I pick up the glass.

"Are you going to call Mark and tell him about it or go back and see him?"

"I'll call him here in a minute. I might go back down there, too, after I finish with the Snake Lady."

She laughs. "I'd like to go along. He's a good guy, Boone."

"Yeah, he is."

So, what do we do now?"

I look at her. "What do you mean?"

"I mean, it's about six-thirty, maybe a quarter til. Do you want to think about eating something, you want to talk, you know, what do we do now?"

"Well," I say, "the one thing I know I need to do right now is feed Frankie. It's just about her suppertime." I get up, fill her dish, and sit back down. Molly watches Frankie for a minute and then turns back to me.

"So what all did she say? I heard a lot of it, but I couldn't catch it all."

"She's really pissed off at Claire, and is bound and determined to get Hannah out of foster care."

"Is that a good idea? Sorry, not my family, not my business."

"Hell, as far as I'm concerned you are family. And I don't think it's a good idea, at least right now. I mean, she's in some kind of shelter for women trying to get away from bad husbands or whatever."

"Family," she says, real soft, and she's got a funny look in her eye.

"What?"

"Nothing. So you think she ought to wait, or not try at all?"

"I don't know, darlin', it was just the one phone call. I mean, she sounds better than I remember, when Daddy was around, but I don't know. I just can't tell yet."

Her stomach growls and she puts her hand over it. "Maybe you ought to feed me, too."

I grin at her and say, "I guess I could eat something. Want me to go pick up a pizza or sandwiches or something, or call Sylvia and see when she's putting supper on the table?"

"Actually, I told Gram not to expect us for supper," Molly says. "I thought this might take a while, and you know how she is about not letting food get cold, or having to reheat it."

I nod. "So, pizza, deli sandwiches, burgers and fries? You pick something and I'll go get it."

Molly says burgers, and there's a place about three miles away that we both like, so I make the trip and we settle back on the couch.

"Next week, I'm making a coffee table," I say. "It'll be ugly as sin, but sturdy."

She nods. Her mouth is too full to answer me. I take another bite and say, "One thing I know I need to do. I need to go see Hannah. After we eat I'll call Mark and then Mrs. Cooperton, see if Momma has talked to Hannah yet."

Chapter Twenty-Eight

We make it to Mark's office without running into Betty this time. He's got a book open on his desk, but he closes it when he sees us standing in the doorway.

"Come in," he says. "So, you need anything?"

"Man, the last time you sent me for coffee I came back and Molly was crying," I say. "No way I'm falling for that again."

He holds his hands up. "No deep conversations without you this time, I promise." He's smiling. "I'll even go get the coffee this time if you two want anything."

"We're good," I say.

He settles into his chair. "How did it go with your mother?"

I look at Molly. She's got her hand on top of Frankie's head, just resting it there, and she's looking at Mark. She turns her head, sees me looking at her, and says, "I was there, sweetie, but it's your story. You should be the one who tells it."

"I know, I know. Just trying to think how to start."

I look back over at Mark. "She called right at six, maybe a minute or two after." I tell him about her crying, and how mad she is at Claire, and how she says she's over Jake and in a shelter, and what she plans to do about Hannah.

"Can she do that?" I ask. "I mean, she doesn't have a place of her own or anything like that."

"They'll look at everything, of course," Mark says. "I can tell you that most of the time a state, whether it's Tennessee or some other, will try very hard to keep children out of foster care if they can, and, if they have to put a child in the system they try to return them to their birth family if that's possible. I don't know about your mother's case. They will certainly entertain the request if she decides to follow through with it and make a formal petition to have custody returned to her."

"What if she really likes where she is?" I'm thinking of the phone call at Christmas. I haven't heard my sister that happy in a really long time, and she'd only been there a little while.

Mark shakes his head. "I don't think that will be much of a factor here, Boone. She's what, eleven or twelve? This is her mother, asking her to come back. I would be very surprised if a child Hannah's age would say no to that."

While I'm thinking about that, Molly says, "Did you know Boone's mother before she left?"

"No," Mark shakes his head. "I met Boone when I was preparing for Gamaliel's funeral. He hadn't been told about his passing, and was still reeling from that shock when I drafted him to speak at the service. He did great, by the way. The other residents were still talking about it a month later. But that was well after his family had fallen apart and he was fending for himself."

He looks over at me and I say to Molly, "Remember I told you once that I had threatened to kick his ass and never followed through with it? I made that threat right after the service, for dragging me up there. I think he said he'd have to take that beating, because he'd do it again. Right, Mark?"

Mark has a big smile on his face. "Right. I still hold to that."

Molly looks from me to Mark and back again. "You two are quite a pair, you know that?"

Mark grins. "I'm going to take that as high praise, my dear." He finishes his coffee and says, "I'll be right back. I need a refill."

He leaves the room and Molly looks around. She points to the picture Mark's brother gave him, the one that's a whole bunch of little pictures of people from when Mark was growing up. "What's that, sweetie?"

I look where she's pointing. "You need to get Mark to tell you that story. I couldn't tell it right."

"I will. Maybe he'll tell me why you and Frankie are in it."

"What?"

She rolls over to it. "See? It's not part of the original, but that little picture stuck under the frame in the corner? That's you and Frankie, isn't it?"

"I was wondering if one of you would notice that." Mark is standing in the doorway.

Molly is blocking his way, being so close to the picture, so he slides behind me and goes around the other side of his desk. He looks at me.

"Surprised?"

I nod.

"You shouldn't be. Remember the common thread among all those people?"

Molly says, "I don't know about this picture, and Boone wouldn't tell me. He said he couldn't do it justice and I should ask you."

Mark tells her the story of how he got the picture as a graduation present from his brother when he finished seminary. He tells her about Reginald, and some of the other people in the picture, and that now he thinks it might be the best present he's ever gotten from anybody.

"All those people," he tells Molly, "not worrying about getting recognized or being important, just paying attention and, when they had a choice to make, choosing to do the right thing. Just that. No big deal, until you add it all up. Then it's maybe the biggest deal there is."

She's looking at the picture. "And the picture of my sweetie and Frankie? I think I already know, but I'd like to hear you tell me."

"It started with that talk at the funeral," Mark says. "I thought right then there was something about Boone. When he moved onto the grounds and started collecting stories from all these old people, I knew. You never realized, did you," he says to me, "how much it meant to those people to have somebody just listen to them? Just hear them? Like I said a minute ago, it was no big deal, until you added it all up. Then it was maybe the biggest deal there was for these people.

"You thought that job was a handout, didn't you?" I nod. "You could not have been more mistaken."

I don't know what to say to that, until I look at Molly and see tears in her eyes. "Dammit, Mark, you said you wouldn't make her cry this time."

"Hush," says Molly.

"I've been thinking for a while that it's part of my job to add to this beautiful gift my brother gave me," Mark says. "You and Frankie won't be the only ones I add, but I can't think of a better pair to start with."

"Can we talk about something else?" I'm pretty embarrassed right now.

Mark starts laughing, and so does Molly. I try not to, but in just a second I give up, and we're all laughing like fools.

It takes us a minute to get over that little spell, and Molly rolls back over to where she was, in front of Mark's desk, and I pull the chair up beside her.

"I'm going to call Hannah tomorrow," I say. "You got any advice for me? I'm not sure how much she knows already."

"That complicates things a bit." Mark takes a sip of his coffee. "You don't want to be the one who springs all this on her. Maybe a few minutes with Mrs. Cooperton before she calls Hannah to the phone?"

I nod. "That makes sense. I figure she'll know something already and maybe she can tell me how Hannah's doing. This is big stuff, bigger for her than me. Momma's not coming to get me, and I wouldn't go if she did. I've got it too good."

"Sometimes, sweetie, you say exactly the right thing." Molly pats me on the arm.

We finally get off the serious stuff and spend a few minutes just talking about this and that. Mark acts like he's got all the time in the world, and he and Molly are hitting it off great.

Before I know it it's time for us to leave. "If we don't get on the road," I say, "Sylvia will have to reheat supper."

"We absolutely cannot have that," says Molly. "I hate to leave, Mark, but we need to get out of here. Gram is particular about mealtime."

He nods. "I had a granny like that once. Boone, call me and tell me about your call to Hannah."

On the way back Molly keeps patting me on the leg, and when I look at her she just smiles and says, "Watch the road, sweetie. I'd like to get there in one piece."

Sylvia is still at the stove when we come into the kitchen, and Molly says, "Wait until I tell you what Mark has on his wall!"

"All right, I'm out of here," I say. "I can't go through that twice in one afternoon."

Molly looks hurt. "Well, then, I'll have to tell her after you leave. You need to stay for supper, Boone. You've got the last day with the Snake Lady tomorrow. You'll need your strength to battle all those snakes."

Frankie and I leave not long after dessert. I need to think about everything that's happened today, and I need to think about what I'm going to say when I call Hannah tomorrow.

Chapter Twenty-Nine

I get finished with the Snake Lady a little early and I'm back home by the middle of the afternoon. I decide to go ahead and call Hannah, even though I don't have any idea what I'm going to say.

Mrs. Cooperton answers the phone right away and says, "Oh, I'm sorry, Boone, but Hannah's doing schoolwork right now. She'll be done around four if you want to call back."

"Actually, Mrs. Cooperton, I was hoping I could talk to you for a minute. If that's okay."

Her voice gets real serious. "Of course, Boone. Is something wrong?"

I'll bet she doesn't know about Momma. I don't know how to ease into this, so I just jump in.

"Ma'am, I got a phone call from Mark, the preacher at the home where I used to work, and he told me I was going to get a phone call from my mother." I hear noise, like she's closing a door or something. "So day before yesterday, she called me. I was just wondering if Hannah had heard from her, or if you had."

There's a long silence, and then she says, "I'm very glad you wanted to talk to me first, Boone. What exactly did your mother say about Hannah? I mean, I'm sure the two of you talked about you, but that's private, and I don't want to pry. If there's something I need to know about Hannah, though, I'd appreciate it very much if you'd tell me."

For a second I'm getting mad, thinking it's none of her damn business what my Momma said about Hannah, but I realize right away that it is her business, since she's taking care of Hannah. It'll be her that's right in the middle of it, whatever it is, if Momma follows through on what she said.

"Well, ma'am, she was real mad about her sister Claire, that's my Aunt Claire, where Hannah was staying, about Claire giving her up to the foster care people. She was talking about getting Hannah back."

"I see."

Her voice is different than any other time I've talked to her. Like a robot, kind of.

"She wanted to know if it was a good place, and I would have told her yes, but she didn't give me a chance. It seems to me like Hannah's pretty happy with you all."

"Thank you for that, Boone. I have to say, I'm surprised to hear about this from you. Usually it comes from someone with the state."

"Well, I don't think she's done anything about it yet, and she did say it might be a while. So she might not have done anything, you know, official."

"I see." She's still ice cold. "So this may be just your mother wishing that she had her daughter back instead of planning to take some kind of action."

"Yes, ma'am, I think it's more, you know, it was the first time she had talked to me in a long time, and some of what we talked about was, like you said, private. The stuff about Hannah, it might be too soon to worry about it, and I think I might have made a mistake telling you."

"No, no, you did not make a mistake. I would much rather know in advance than get a surprise call from your mother. Did she say she was going to call here?"

"No, ma'am, she had to get off to go to some kind of meeting. She said she'd call me back soon, but she didn't say anything about calling Hannah or Aunt Claire either one."

"I see."

I can tell she's either real worried or real mad. It's a good minute before she says anything.

"Here's what we need to do, Boone. I'm going to tell Hannah you called, but she was doing school work and you said that you'd call back in a day or two. That will give me time to check with the case worker and see if she's heard anything about a formal request. I'll tell Hannah that you said you had heard from your mother, and that she's doing well. Is that true, is she doing well?"

"She sounded pretty good, except for crying a bunch, but like I said, it's been a long time since we talked."

"I think a few tears would be very appropriate. Do you know where she's living? Is she in Tennessee?"

I tell her somewhere in Illinois, not far from Chicago.

"I can't tell you how glad I am that you wanted to talk to me first, Boone. I've been a foster parent for quite a few years, and children, even the ones who like to pretend they're really tough, are fragile, especially early in placement.

"I like your sister, and she is adjusting well to living here with us. If she thinks her mother is coming by to get her next week or next month, though, it can be very damaging if that doesn't happen. So if you'll give me the chance to find out where we are officially, I can help Hannah deal with the fact that her mother is possibly back in the picture."

I think I'm supposed to be mad about her kind of taking over here, but I'm not. I'm really glad I don't have to figure out what to say to Hannah and what to keep from her. This is a lot better.

"Thanks, Mrs. Cooperton. I really wasn't sure about calling, or what to say or not say, and if you know how this is supposed to work, that's better, I think."

"I agree, Boone, and, again, thank you for giving me some advance notice of this possible change in Hannah's situation. Give me a couple of days and then call back. I'll tell you what I've found out and then you can talk to Hannah."

"I will. I wanted to ask you, how's Sam? You know, the girl that was so scared of Frankie? I didn't mean to scare her."

"She's fine, Boone. I can't tell you anything about why she was so scared, but I can tell you it had nothing to do with either you or your dog. I'm sure Frankie is a lovely pet. Sam's history makes it problematic to have large dogs around her. I hope you understand that I can't say more than that."

"I get it. I'm glad she's okay. I'll talk to you in a couple of days."

After I hang up I mix an S&S and sit out on the porch. Frankie comes outside with me for a few minutes and goes back in to her corner of the living room.

I wonder if Momma is really going to try to get Hannah away from Mrs. Cooperton. It's been so long since I talked to her that I'm not sure how to take all the stuff she said. She was mad at Claire, that's for sure. She sounds stronger than any time after my brother died and she just sort of gave up, so that's a good thing.

"Hey, Frankie, I wonder what Momma will say when she meets you and finds out what your name is?"

Frankie thumps her tail but other than that doesn't answer me.

I wonder if Momma will ever meet Frankie. I'm not going to travel up to Illinois to see her, and I don't know if she's coming down here or whether she's done with Tennessee. If she asks me to come up there to see her I don't know what I'll say. I don't know how far away Chicago is.

I get Melvin's map out of the truck and take it inside. I spread it out on the kitchen counter and look for Chicago.

It looks like it'd be an eight or nine hour drive to get to Chicago. Might be less to wherever she is, if she stays there. She might move again, though. Who the hell knows?

I'm all mixed up here. I guess I was glad to hear from Momma. I know I'm still pissed off that she just left me and took off with Hannah. I'm mad about her helping Jake steal the truck, but if I'm being fair about it I guess she probably thought it was Daddy's truck, and she wouldn't think twice about stealing from him if she thought she could get away with it.

I wonder what she's going to think about all the stuff I've done in the last four years or so. If I tell her. She might be okay with Gamaliel, but not the shine making lessons. She would have been crazy about Nancy, I'm sure. Mark, now, she would not have been okay with me getting to be such good friends with a black guy. And Billie, well, she might have smacked me right across the face for that. I'm sure that would have been across the line for her.

I don't know what she'll think about Molly. She might be one of those people that sees the chair instead of the person. Probably.

"And that's a damn shame," I say to Frankie. "You and me, we both know how great Molly is."

Frankie's up and trotting toward me, looking around for Molly.

"She's not here, girl," I say, laughing. "I wish she was. She could help me sort this out."

I pick up the phone and call her.

"Hey, sweetie," she says. "Did you call Hannah?"

I fill her in on my call to Mrs. Cooperton, and she says, "I think you are probably right. She knows how this kind of thing works, and I don't think giving her a day or two to find things out is a bad idea at all."

"Damn, I wish you were over here."

"Me, too, sweetie, but it's a little late. If you finished your job maybe we can get some lunch tomorrow."

"I did, and lunch sounds like a great idea. I'll call you tomorrow morning."

"Okay. Love you, sweetie."

"Love you too, Molly."

I hang up and think, man, she is one great girl. As soon as I think that I hear her say, woman. One great woman.

Chapter Thirty

It's two weeks before Momma calls back, and I miss it because I'm out in the yard and the phone is sitting on the kitchen counter. She doesn't leave a message or anything, but it's the same number that she called from the first time we talked.

"I hope everything's okay," I say to Molly. She's here to eat some lunch with me and Frankie, and we're planning a short drive in the afternoon. I've got two jobs coming up next week, both of them at least a couple of days, so it's a full week for me.

"I'd say give it a few days," she says. "Too soon to worry, I think."

The next time I hear from her is almost a week later, and she sounds really good. I guess she got all the crying out of the way on that first call. The thing that hasn't changed is how mad she is at Claire, and I have to tell her a bunch of times that

I can't get in the middle of this, it's got to be her fight. Claire didn't talk to me about it besides the threat on my voicemail, didn't ask for any help with Hannah, and I don't even know what it was she was supposed to have done. She finally gets it and says she'll deal with Claire.

When I ask her if she's talked to Hannah, she doesn't answer for a second.

"I talked to that lady Coppersomething, and she said Hannah was doing good and I shouldn't say anything about getting her back until I knew for sure when that was going to be."

"I've talked to Mrs. Cooperton a few times, Momma," I say, "and she seems okay to me. I think she's taking good care of Hannah."

"I guess. Well, anyway, I talked to Hannah a couple of times and I did what the lady wanted, I didn't say anything about taking her back. It was really hard, Boone, really hard."

"I know, Momma. I really think she'll be okay there until you're ready to get her back."

I can tell Momma's not real happy about this, and I don't know how long it's going to be before she starts working on Hannah. She sounds good, though, and that's what I tell Molly after she hangs up.

"That's the only thing you can do, sweetie," she says. "It can't be your fight. Hannah's in one state, your mother's in another one, and you're just now figuring out what you're going to do with your own life. You did right by telling her it's her job to set things right with Hannah, and with Claire."

"I don't know if it'll ever be right between those two," I say. "I don't know that I've ever heard Momma that mad about anything. I mean, except when Frankie died.

"Anyway, she's sounding better, and the last time I talked to Hannah she sounded good, too, so I guess I'm glad about all that."

Molly doesn't say anything for a couple of minutes. Then she rolls over to the coffee table I finished last week and picks up her glass of tea, takes a sip, and sets it back down. She knocks on the table a couple of times and says, "Sturdy, but not entirely ugly. Definitely not ugly as sin. I think you're losing your style, sweetie."

I grin. "Maybe, but it's still a long damn way from fancy woodwork."

"Gram has a couple of jobs for you when you get done with these next two," she says. "I don't think it's anything big."

"Tell her I'll put her on the list," I say.

By the next month I'm having to tell people it'll be a while before I can get to them. I guess people are either too busy or too old to do this kind of stuff themselves, and that's fine with me. I can work a week or two and keep the next week free and still get enough money to make the rent and stuff. Gamaliel's money is mostly still sitting there, and I'd like to keep it that way as long as I can.

I'm cleaning out the truck from one of my trash hauling jobs when my phone rings. It's Ralph, and for a minute I think, oh hell, did I forget to pay my rent this month, but that's not what he's calling about.

"Hey, Boone, I wanted to let you know we had a family meeting last night about the property."

Here we go, I think.

"Just wanted to give you a heads up. We're not going to do anything this year, but next year we're probably going to be talking to a developer. I don't know if you've noticed or not, but some of the farms not all that far away from you are getting sold and split up for subdivisions and that kind of thing. I like having the rent income myself, but when we all got together everybody else was thinking a big check once and split it up, instead of a little one every month that's not hardly worth the trouble to divide. "

"I appreciate you letting me know, Ralph. So when do you need me out of here?"

"Most likely not until next spring, and I told them we'd have to give you a couple of month's notice to find another place. You're a good renter, and we wouldn't just dump you out on the street."

"That's good. I mean, it's a good place to live, and I got to tell you I hate the thought of leaving. But I get it, Ralph, just let me know. Give me as much notice as you can."

"We will. See you later."

I hang up and tell Frankie, "It was good while it lasted, girl, but I'm thinking we need to start looking pretty soon instead of waiting on them to give us a month or two."

I'm not real worried about it. Since I'm all over the place doing these little jobs for people, I can think of three or four For Rent signs that I've seen just in the last month or so.

"You're moving?" That night at dinner, Molly sounds about half scared and half mad. "You can't move!"

"Not my idea," I say. "Ralph had some kind of family meeting about it. Not until next year, is what he said, but I figure I need to start looking around. I like it around here, I've got work around here, and I can't see getting too far away from you, so I don't want to wait until the last minute. Living out of the back of the truck is okay, but I've gotten kind of spoiled, having a bed and a kitchen and all that."

She turns to Sylvia. "Gram, we can't let this happen! You need to talk to Ralph."

Sylvia shakes her head. "It's not just Ralph, dear. If it was I could maybe talk him out of it, but it's his whole family. Besides, you heard what Boone said. He said he's not going to get too far away from you, and I've seen you two together. I can guarantee you he'll stay close by."

"That's right," I say. "You're not getting rid of me, darlin'. I know when I've got it good."

I'm not sure she believes me, and she's real quiet all through supper.

"I'll tell you what," I say. "Next week, when I've got some free time, you come with me and Frankie while we go out looking. You can help me pick out the new place."

That gets a smile, but then she turns to Sylvia.

"He can move in here, right? He's here most of the time anyway. There. Problem solved."

Sylvia starts to say something, but I jump in first.

"I'll tell you, Molly, one of the first thoughts I had was doing that very thing. But I decided that wouldn't be right, and I'll tell you why.

"I've told you some about what's happened to me before I met you, right?" She nods. Her eyes are looking way down into mine. "You know I lived at home with my folks, and then I lived in Gamaliel's house, and then I lived at the home, in that little house they had on the property, and then I lived out of the back of my truck. Until I ran across the house I'm in now, I never lived in my own place. This house," I wave my hand around, "is a great house. It's Sylvia's, and it's yours, but it's not mine. When we're out riding around or whatever, and I can say, 'Why don't we go over to my place?' that's a real big deal for me. I've thought about sharing a home with you, and I can't think of anything better. I'd like for that to happen sometime, but I think I need to know what it's like to have my own place, just for a while."

I drop my head down and stare at the floor. "I know my friends would call me a purebred fool for putting up any kind of a fight about moving in with a smart, fine looking woman like you."

Frankie comes over and sits up real close. I reach out and rest my hand on her head. "I figure a couple of hours from now when I'm sitting on my couch, I'll be calling myself the same thing."

Sylvia laughs. "You are the most surprising young man I've ever run across. Molly, dear, I don't know what you saw in him the first time you met, but you certainly have good taste in men."

"I know," says Molly.

We don't find anything in the next couple of weeks, but it's a lot of fun looking, and having Molly along is great. She knows a bunch of the back roads around here, and I know I want a place out in the country, so we work together pretty well.

We're sitting on the couch at my place one afternoon, sipping and talking about the houses we've seen this past week. I take a sip, set the glass on the coffee table, and turn to Molly.

"You remember me talking about Raymond and Charlotte?"

She frowns. "Not really. Are they friends of yours?"

When I start the story of the three guys in the parking lot at the Okefenokee Swamp, she says, "Oh, yeah. I remember them. Really rich, just

cruising around the country, Raymond had that
fruity moonshine that you almost spit out the first
time you tasted it."

"That's them," I say.

"What made you think of them?"

"Well, I was on my way to drop in on them
when I got turned around by that mess with
Claire and Hannah. I ended up coming back down
11W, and saw that For Rent sign, and, well, you
know the rest."

Molly looks puzzled. "So?"

"So I called Raymond yesterday, just to say hi
and see what they're up to. Turns out they're at
home in Virginia for a month, and he invited me
and Frankie to come visit them next week. I told
him I might be bringing my girlfriend along. That
is, if you're interested."

"I am. Definitely."

I nod. "Good. I'll call Raymond back and let him
know."

End of Book Five

Author's Note

Along with my wife Suzanne, who is invaluable as the first reader of all my books, catching the mistakes that I miss because I auto-correct as I'm reading my own work, I'd like to thank my new friend Joel Simmons. He not only helped me with my characterization of Molly, he understood one of the main points of the story immediately, which was very gratifying.